CH0086936

Score to Love

AN INTERNATIONAL SPORTS ROMANCE

JOHANA GAVEZ

To all the readers that have opened a space in their TBR pile for my books. Thank you for the support, the positive feedback and, most of all, for letting my stories come alive in your minds.

Contents

Chapter One

CAMILA SAT ALONE IN the home cinema at her dad's Beverly Hills mansion. It was her home too, but she struggled to use that word for the plain white walls and modern structure surrounding her. It was simply where she'd been staying for the past couple of weeks after graduating from UCLA while she waited to join the Houston Starlight as one of their draft picks.

She couldn't wait to leave LA. To have a place of her own again, away from her parents. Most of all, she couldn't wait to show the world what she was capable of and to take her place on an NWSL team. Being the sixteenth overall draft pick wasn't bad, but she wanted to be more than just another player.

Camila took a long sip of ice water and narrowed her eyes at the giant screen in front of her. She wanted to be a fundamental part of the United States women's national soccer team. She wanted to raise trophies and score decisive goals to give her team a big win, not watch them on TV. Instead, she was sitting on her ass while the players good enough to make the team led it to another win.

It was only a friendly game, but it stung to know she still wasn't good enough to be there. Camila knew she was young and had plenty of time to show her worth, to impress the head coach enough to be called to the team. But she longed to be there already.

She straightened up in her seat and moved to the edge of the black leather chair. Her attention shifted to a petite woman wearing a yellow and green jersey and the number ten on her back. When her team recovered the ball, she crossed the entire field before anyone could stop her, eluding the two lone defenders in her way with a precise dribble she didn't even have to slow down to make. The quick counterattack from the Brazilian team almost ended with a goal to tie the match at two per side, but a miraculous save by the goalkeeper kept the US team leading.

"That was a close call for the United States team," the commentator said. "Antonia Carvalho is the kind of player that can change an entire match in a second, and she almost did after that imprecise pass by Johnson. There's a reason Brazil called Carvalho to defend its colors. Several international teams are looking to sign her, despite the fact that she's only nineteen years old."

Nineteen years old. Two years younger than Camila, yet already the star of her team.

All while Camila struggled to be noticed.

By the time the match ended fifteen minutes later, the glass in her hand was empty. She turned off the TV, deciding it was better to put her time to good use and head to the gym or go for a run. That was the plan, at least. But when she walked into the kitchen, she ran into her dad.

"Hola, cariño," he said, taking a sip through the metal straw of his ever-present mate. "Saw the team won."

Camila returned his greeting with a tight-lipped smile and shook her head from side to side when he pushed the cup made of calabash gourd in her direction. She'd never been able to handle the traditional tea-like beverage, no matter how much her father gushed about its properties and swore it was way more potent than the coffee she preferred. She may be half Uruguayan, but mate was certainly an acquired tasted she would never get.

"Yeah, it was a great match. The Brazilian team didn't make it easy."

"Don't be upset. You'll be there next time."

She nodded, trying to ignore the sinking feeling in her stomach. She was grateful for her dad's words but also painfully aware of the fact she was far from being considered for the national team. Yes, she had great numbers while she played for UCLA. Good enough to be drafted. But her biggest claim to fame was being the daughter of Ricardo Sánchez, the famous Uruguay star center-forward. That's who people thought of when they heard her name.

Maybe she should have listened to her mom when she insisted on taking Camila to casting calls and modeling agencies as a teenager. But then she'd be the daughter of supermodel Claudia Davis. Not much of a difference. No matter what she did, she'd always live in the shadow of her parents.

"That's the plan, yeah," she said quickly before her dad noticed her dark mood.

"I talked to Franco today. He's looking forward to having you on the team."

Camila suppressed a groan. Part of her hated that Franco Medina, one of her dad's best friends, coached the team that picked her.

"I'll go to Houston with you to help you get settled and have a word with him," her dad said.

"That's not necessary."

"Of course it is." He walked out of the kitchen. For him, the conversation was over.

Camila sighed and grabbed another bottle of water from the fridge. She really needed that run now.

Antonia ran along the beach, advancing with the worn-out football that was glued to her side as if it were part of her own body. Sometimes, an irregular mound of sand made it jump, but she always controlled it before it got away.

The sand, the smell of the ocean, the ball under her feet—it all reminded Antonia of a simpler time. A time when she didn't worry about money for rent or food because she didn't know there was a reason to worry. Her life had been a continuous loop of running around on the beach and kicking a ball back and forth with her brother. She'd never been as happy as she was then.

At first, she wasn't sure where she was going. Her only goal was to enjoy the few hours she had left in Florianópolis before a plane took her away to a new world. She wasn't surprised when she ended up in front of the resort where her mom had worked for so many years while she and Leo played. There had been only four constants in her life growing up: football, her brother, the beach, and the resort. It was natural for her to want to enjoy them one last time before leaving.

Instead of going in and saying goodbye to the people who'd been like a second family for so many years,

Antonia sat in the sand and stared at the horizon. Tourists wandered around her as they looked for the perfect spot to tan, but she didn't move, unbothered by the kids who ran around playing, yelling, and splashing like she used to on that same beach. They looked at her football and bickered, probably trying to decide who would be brave enough to ask her for it. When the smallest of the bunch walked toward her, she smiled. His torn shirt and ragged shorts reminded her of herself as a kid, always on the beach, always eager to play football.

"Would you mind if we borrowed your ball?" he said, eyes full of expectation.

The others watched in a huddle a few steps away, which made it impossible for her to say no. Not that she would ever deny anyone the joy of playing football.

She grabbed the ball and stood up. "I have a better idea. If you can keep the ball from touching the ground longer than I can, you can keep it."

"Really?"

She nodded, and the boy's eyes brightened at the possibility. She had loved that ball for years, but there was limited space in her suitcase, and she knew they would enjoy it more. Even a worn-out ball would give them hours or even months of entertainment.

She threw the ball in the air and caught it with her thigh, then her foot, back up to her chest and thigh.

The amount of force she needed to apply to make the ball soar into the air to the perfect height came naturally. She'd done it so many times there was no need to think. As long as she kept her eye on the ball, her body always knew when and how to move to maintain it in play.

Out of the corner of her eye, she saw the group of kids move closer, mouths agape. She couldn't resist the urge to show off a little. She kicked the ball harder, high enough that it went over her head, and caught it between her shoulder blades. Without missing a beat, she dropped the ball and turned around to catch it again with her foot.

She kicked the ball toward the kid who had approached her. "Your turn."

He shook his head and stared at the ball for a long minute before pushing it in the air with the tip of his foot. He limited his movements to passing the ball from one foot to the other and occasionally hit it with his thigh. It wasn't fancy, but he was good enough to control the ball. He only needed to keep it off the ground longer than Antonia, and nobody said anything about having to do riskier movements. He was smart, she would give him that. As he got closer to the number of times she hit the ball, the kids started jumping around while counting.

"Thirty-two, thirty-three, thirty-four, thirty-five, thirty-six!"

He stopped after doing two more kicks, grabbed the ball, and looked at her, probably expecting her to go back on her word. She had only done thirty-six touches because she stopped, not because she dropped the ball, but it didn't matter. She always intended to give them the ball no matter what happened.

"It's yours," she said.

As soon as the words left her mouth, the group of kids ran away, kicking the ball between them and laughing. It warmed her heart to know she could bring them happiness with so little. She turned around, ready to return home to finish packing, when the small kid ran back to her.

"Do you want to play?" he said, catching his breath.

She was about to say no. She'd promised Leo they would have lunch together, and it was getting late, but she couldn't resist one last game on the beach where she'd first learned to play.

There was no better way to play football than barefoot on the beach, with the heat and breeze hitting you in the face. She ran toward the boys, and they received her with shouts and screams of joy, both teams fighting for her services. The only way to stop the discussion was to promise to play one game with one team and then switch to the other.

She scored a couple of goals and won both games. When she left, the kids made her promise to come back and play with them again. She did. And she would. She didn't know when she would return, but when she did, this beach would be her first stop.

Houston was her future, but Florianópolis would always be her home.

The aroma of fish, onions, and peppers filled Antonia's senses when she opened the door. She recognized the smell. Leo had to be cooking one of her favorite dishes, the tainha na telha that her mother always reserved for special occasions like their birthdays.

She was going to miss her brother. Not because of the cooking, even if he was great at it, but because they only had each other now that their mother was gone. Although Antonia was leaving to make her dream—their dream—a reality, to follow in the footsteps of Marta and Formiga, she couldn't help but feel a small flicker of guilt.

He turned around at the sound of the door and flashed that bright, toothy grin everyone loved. "Right on time! Food is almost ready."

"It smells amazing."

Antonia sat at the small counter that served as their dining table and watched him while he ran around the kitchen. Everyone always said he looked just like their mom, with his golden-brown hair and hazel eyes. But unlike their mother, he never lost his childlike cheerfulness.

Antonia looked more like her dad. She'd never met him, but she had to look like him. Her curly black hair and dark brown eyes always set her apart from her brother and her mom. She'd love to have at least a picture to compare herself to, but her mom never cared to talk about their dad and hadn't kept any mementos from their time together. He'd existed, and he'd left them. That's all they needed to know about him.

Antonia didn't blame her mom for not wanting to talk about him. It had been hard for her, working sixteen hours a day, alone with two kids. There had been little energy left to mourn someone who didn't want them.

When her mom died, Antonia feared that Leo would grow to resent her for being forced to become the head of the household and take care of her, but he never did. He stopped playing football on the beach with her and found a job. He made sure she had something to eat every day—or most of them, at least—and always found a pair of boots for her to play in, no matter how fast she wore them out.

Now it was time for her to take care of him. Being a professional football player wasn't only her dream, it was the only way she could pay him back for everything he'd done.

With a huge smile on his face, Leo set an entire beautifully roasted fish on the table and sat in front of her. "I stuffed it with shrimp. I know that's your favorite."

"It is." She tried to flash him a smile of her own, but she knew it didn't reach her eyes.

"Why the long face? We're celebrating!"

"I know. I just . . . I'm going to miss you."

He embraced her and ruffled her hair in the exact way he knew she hated. "Aw, and here I was thinking you couldn't wait to get rid of me."

"I mean, I won't miss sharing a cramped apartment with you and your smelly clothes. But you're not the worst company."

The truth was, she'd never lived her life without him in it. Yes, she was independent. She had walked alone to training since she was twelve, because Leo couldn't work and babysit her at the same time. Around the same age, she had started doing their laundry, and she had traveled plenty of times with her teams. She could take care of herself, but the thought of not having his bright eyes greeting her every morning pained her.

"I'm going to miss you too," he said, bumping her shoulder. "But you're going to be living your dream, and it's not like you'll forget about me. I'll keep working hard at the resort, and I've been thinking about applying to a culinary school. Before you know it, I'll be an international chef, and I'll be able to go visit you."

She nodded. "You'll join me soon, I promise," she said, determined to make it happen.

Chapter Two

CAMILA TRIED TO HIDE her face when her parents insisted on taking her to her first practice. She was a professional soccer player, but there she was, with her dad and mom walking beside her as they arrived at the stadium.

"Dad, I don't think it's necessary for you to talk with the coach," she said in one last attempt to shake them off. She knew it wouldn't work. She had tried to talk her dad out of coming to the first official training session for weeks, and every time he refused to listen.

"Franco and I go a long way back. I promise that me being here will only help you."

That was the problem. She didn't want him to help. Of course, she couldn't say that to him. He'd always managed her career and never understood why it bothered her so much when he tried to use the gravitas that being a former world champion gave him in her favor. He always felt he knew better. She bit her tongue to prevent a scathing remark from escaping, took a deep breath to clear her thoughts, and tried again to explain to her dad why she didn't want him here.

"You can catch up some other time. I don't want other players to think I'll get preferential treatment because you're my dad. That wouldn't be the best way to start my relationship with my new teammates."

Her dad stopped walking and turned around to look at her. He cupped her face, a gesture that made Camila feel like a little kid. "I'm not trying to get you preferential treatment. You're here because you've earned it and worked hard for it. But it doesn't hurt to remind him that you're my daughter. He would be a fool to not make you a starter when you have my genes."

Any remaining hope she had of him seeing where she was coming from vanished. She nodded, not because she agreed with his reasoning but because she gave up. If there was no way to get her parents to leave, she would have to suck it up and make her teammates forget it happened.

"Now that that's settled, let's take a picture to remember our baby's first day with a professional team," her mom said, pulling her into a hug.

Her dad was one thing—at least he was an ex-soccer player and coach. As much as Camila hated having him here, it made sense. The fact that her mom also tagged along was another matter altogether. She was never around growing up, always too busy with work and traveling the world modeling. But somehow she always showed up when there was potential for a photo op. The last thing Camila wanted was a picture that she knew wouldn't end up in the family album but would instead be shared with her mom's legion of fans. She extricated herself from under her mom's arm and increased her pace.

"Let's move it. I don't want to be late."

As soon as they made it inside the stadium, she left her parents behind to let them wander around and do whatever it was they wanted to do, while she headed to the locker room. As she sat in front of the locker with her name on it, she felt like she belonged for the first time. Like she deserved to be there. She didn't want that feeling to go away, but she knew as soon as she stepped on the field and saw her dad making nice with the coach, it would.

The locker room was safe. If it were up to her, she would have stayed as long as possible. But there was one thing that scared her more than the entire team seeing her parents parading around, and that was getting on the coach's bad side by being late.

With a sigh, she stood up. She'd only taken two steps toward the door when the burning feeling of someone looking at her made her turn around. Brown eyes stared back at her from the opposite corner of the locker room.

Camila sized the other girl up, lingering a second or two longer than necessary on the exposed abs and toned arms. She felt no guilt over enjoying the view, since she was only returning the favor. Despite being caught and overtly ogled, the other girl didn't look away. She finished looking Camila up and down as if Camila weren't staring right back at her.

It was hard to tell from afar, but she seemed small, shorter than her for sure—shorter than most on the team, she assumed. Which meant she was extremely talented if she had scored a spot on the team. The Starlight were a new franchise with a lot of money invested in them, and they'd spared no expense to get some of the best players. There was something familiar about the wild curly black hair framing her face, but Camila couldn't place it. She didn't come from the NCAA; she was sure of that, at least.

She looked away first and cursed internally as soon as she did, but she couldn't deal with the intensity of the girl's stare. She should have ignored the situation, turned around, and left like she intended. Camila wasn't sure why she didn't, why she felt compelled to speak up in the middle of the locker room with her future teammates around.

"Are you checking me out?" she said in a tone more accusatory than she intended. She winced when all movement and noise around her stopped, everyone's attention turning to her.

Great. Exactly what she was trying to avoid.

The girl took her sweet time before answering. She stood up and put her shirt on first, then walked up to her. She was even more beautiful up close, with her brown skin almost shining under the fluorescent lights. Camila fought the urge to glance at her plump lips. That would be embarrassing right after she called her out for staring.

"Don't flatter yourself. I was reading the name on your jersey. Sánchez."

There was a hint of an accent in her words that Camila couldn't place. It sounded melodic, almost like a song—and it made the bitterness used to say Camila's last name more evident.

"I guess that explains why Ricardo Sánchez is fluttering around, whispering in the coach's ear."

Any hint of attraction left Camila's body, replaced by a surge of rage. She stepped forward, invading the girl's personal space, nostrils flaring. "Are you implying something?" she said through gritted teeth.

"I don't imply. If I have something to say, I say it."

Camila saw red, but before she could reply, a hand on her shoulder snapped her to her senses. When she turned around, veteran USWNT player Stephanie Brown stood between them with a hand on each of their shoulders.

"Sánchez. Carvalho. We're on the same team. Let's tone it down."

Camila nodded, embarrassed at getting into a fight less than thirty minutes into the season, and especially ashamed that a player she greatly admired had to intervene. They shook hands as a sign of peace. Camila hated how Carvalho's hand was soft and warm, but she hated her smug, condescending look even more. Dealing with her for at least a season was going to be a nightmare.

Antonia had to admit that Sánchez was hot, but she was also entitled and presumptuous—the opposite of her type, no matter how physically attractive she was. Antonia had dealt with people exactly like her in the past, players who swore they were on the team because of their talent and hard work when everybody knew that their family name and money had bought them a spot. Not all of them were poor players, but all of them, without exception, were clueless. Ignorant or pretending to be unaware of their own advantages.

She didn't begrudge them because they were luckier than her. Everyone had to play the hand they were dealt, after all, but she hated the way they pretended they didn't have an advantage. That's why when she got called out for staring, she attacked where she knew it would hurt instead of flirting and admitting she was admiring the view. Maybe it wasn't the best way to start her stay on a new team, but the arrogance in Sánchez's voice had gotten the best of her.

She didn't care if the coach's pet didn't like her. At the end of the day, what counted were the results, and she was sure she played better than anyone on the team.

When Coach Medina separated them into two teams for a practice game, Antonia knew it was her chance to show off.

"Carvalho, López, McCarty, Sánchez, and Jones, you're on team red. Grab a vest."

Antonia ran to the pile of equipment, eager to play. As she grabbed the first vest on top of the pile, another hand pulled the fabric in the opposite direction. She followed the hand up to find herself staring at Sánchez again. For a long, drawn-out moment, neither of them let go; the surprise in Sánchez's eyes morphed into annoyance in a split second, but before she could react, Antonia broke their staring contest and grabbed another vest.

"Carvalho, I know you've played as central forward, winger, and center midfield. I want to test you on midfield first," Coach Medina's voice boomed.

"Sure thing, sir."

Winger was her favorite role, but she would play wherever the coach asked. She knew she could stand out regardless of what position she played. As soon as the ball touched her feet, her focus shifted to the game and nothing else. She forgot about her dislike of Sánchez. The only thing that mattered was winning.

She helped her team score the first goal. Using her speed, she ran down the right side until she almost reached the end of the pitch and then placed a precise high pass to the middle of the small area where Sánchez only needed to touch the ball with the tip of her boot to score. In the heat of the moment, she ran toward Sánchez to celebrate, only for the other girl to turn around and walk away when Antonia got close. López saved her from embarrassment by offering a high-five and a quick hug, but when Antonia saw an opening near Sánchez, she passed the ball to Jones instead—merely by coincidence, of course.

After thirty minutes, she noticed Coach Medina look at his watch, and she realized the practice game would be over soon. Both teams had scored twice, but that wouldn't do. She didn't care if it was practice; she wanted to win.

After recovering the ball in the middle of the pitch, she ran toward the goal, leaving rivals and teammates behind. She was right outside the goal area with two defenders in her way. Out of the corner of her eye, she saw Sánchez appear to her right, behind the defender's back. A well-placed pass would leave Sánchez alone in front of the goalkeeper with a high chance to score. Antonia would usually take the option with a higher possibility of ending in a goal, but in the split second it took her to decide, she opted for trying to score on her own instead of making a pass.

With a fast movement of her feet and waist, she left the two defenders behind. The goalkeeper ran toward her, trying to reduce her angle of shot, but right when the goalkeeper slid down at the ball, Antonia gave a precise kick to send the ball over her body and into the net.

This time, she didn't bother to celebrate. She grabbed the ball from the back of the net and walked to the middle of the pitch as the coach announced the end of the game.

Sánchez looked at her from afar with ice in her eyes.

Camila tried to let it go. She really did. She took a deep breath and counted to one hundred. If stupid Carvalho didn't want to pass the ball to her, it didn't matter. She didn't need her help to prove she was the best forward on the team. She wasn't as fast, and she didn't show off with dribbling skills, but she knew that inside the goal area, nobody was better at scoring. The shape of the net was ingrained in her brain. She could find it even with her eyes closed. She didn't need anyone's help. Not her dad's, and not Carvalho's.

After the practice game, Coach Medina split them into two training groups. He worked on one side of the field, and his assistant coach Megan Hall, legend of the USWNT, worked on the other. Camila was spared from dealing with Carvalho, who was not in her group.

Training with Coach Megan, as she insisted they call her, lifted Camila's spirit. She'd had posters of her on her walls growing up, and maybe even a small crush that helped her discover she was a lesbian as a teenager. At forty years old, Coach Megan had small wrinkles at the edges of her lips and eyes that only made her more attractive. Camila had gotten over her crush years before, but she still held a deep admiration for the woman. Coach Megan had been coaching since her retirement five years before, and in Camila's opinion, she had more than enough credentials to coach any team in the world. It was a crime that sexism

22

kept her an assistant coach, but she would eventually have to take over a team. She was too talented not to become a head coach.

Camila was joined by teammates Stephanie Brown, Samantha Jones, Morgan Press, Kristen Ferrara, Dominique Perdue, and Liz Young on her side of the field. She stood next to Liz while Coach Megan explained the drills she wanted them to do. Liz had been one of Camila's best friends at UCLA. Back when they barely knew each other, they'd shared a drunken kiss born out of a dare at a party. The kiss had such little chemistry, they could only laugh about it. It was an unusual start to a friendship, but without that incident and Liz's natural friendliness, Camila would have missed out on a great best friend. She was almost happier when Houston chose Liz for the team than when she'd been picked herself. For someone like her, who had always struggled to make friends, having Liz with her was invaluable. She was also one of the best defenders in the NCAA, which gave Camila confidence in knowing she was on a winning team.

"Your dad is leaving," Liz whispered close to her ear.

Camila raised her gaze to find him walking in the stands. His sharp black suit stood out against the bright orange of the stadium seats. She couldn't see his expression from that distance, but she could imagine his disapproving scowl. She'd seen it enough times in the past to picture it clearly in her mind.

Everyone ran around her, bringing her back to Earth and exposing the fact she'd missed the end of Coach Megan's instructions. She fell back behind the rest of her teammates and followed their lead, running around the cones placed on the grass to end with a shot on the goal as they did.

For half an hour Camila ran, dribbled, and shot, her focus only on the soccer ball. But as soon as the coach ended the practice, her attention landed on Carvalho. She was laughing loudly, an obnoxious, grating laugh that reached her ears even from the other side of the field. López clearly found whatever Carvalho was saying equally amusing. She was also laughing, with her head thrown back and her arm draped around Carvalho's shoulders as if they'd known each other forever. Camila wasn't sure why it annoyed her so much, but it did.

"Whoa there, tiger, maybe ease up on the dagger eyes," Liz said, walking beside her.

"I've never met someone so infuriating."

"Who? Carvalho? You've known her for like two hours, and only thirty seconds of that was actually talking to each other."

Liz had always been a pacifist. Camila appreciated how patient and understanding Liz was and the way she handled Camila's erratic mood swings was one reason their friendship worked. But for once Camila wished she'd get on her side instead of trying to be the nice guy.

"Those thirty seconds were more than enough. I can't stand her."

Liz laughed softly. "It's our first day, and we're a team. We should try to get along with everyone."

Camila rolled her eyes. "I'd rather keep things professional."

Chapter Three

CAMILA RUSHED TO SHOWER and change when she got to the locker room after practice. She was eager to leave for her team-provided apartment in downtown Houston. The first day of training hadn't gone to plan, and she was looking forward to some alone time at last. Maybe a bubble bath to relax her muscles and help her forget the unpleasant parts of her day.

She was almost done getting dressed when Liz sat next to her.

"You're coming, right?" Liz said, putting a hand on her shoulders.

"Coming to what?"

"The team building party. We're all going to Torchy's for some tacos and then crashing Jones's parents' house in River Oaks. There's a pool."

Camila stopped tying her shoes to look at Liz. "I didn't know there was a party. But no, doesn't seem like the best way to start the season. I'm sure Coach Medina would prefer if we stayed away from parties."

"He knows about it, and he thinks it's a great way to help us get to know each other better and bond. It won't be anything over the top. Music and some food, that's all."

There went Camila's plans for a quiet night at home. She would've rather gone anywhere else, but she couldn't be the only one not attending. Getting along with her teammates probably wouldn't hurt, especially since there was already one she couldn't stand.

"I promised my dad I'd meet him for dinner before he left," she lied. "Text me the address, and I'll meet you there."

The fact that she had to go to the party didn't mean she had to enjoy it or get there on time. Instead of going to Torchy's with the rest of the team, she drove home, made herself dinner, and watched TV. It was only Liz's insistent text messages asking where she was that forced her to get off her ass and get to the party. She hoped that by the time she got there, the party would be almost over.

She couldn't have been more wrong.

As Camila walked inside the house, the sound of chatting mixed with music filled her ears. Every person she encountered on her way to the pool had a red cup in their hands. It was as if she'd traveled back in time to a random college party. Not that she went to many of those. She almost turned around and left before anyone saw her, but Liz waved at her from the other side of the pool and ruined her plan. She was standing with half a dozen of her teammates and all of them turned around to look at Camila, making her escape impossible.

"Alcohol-free beer. Your favorite," Liz said as soon as she joined them, pushing a bottle into her hands.

Camila took a sip of the drink for lack of anything better to do, grateful there were alcohol-free drinks available since she intended to drive home. There was nothing she hated more than being told to relax. Outside of the field, she was fine with blending into the background and letting everyone else take the spotlight. She hoped showing her face was enough to placate her teammates' desire for bonding.

"So, what's your deal with Carvalho?"

She hadn't expected to become the topic of conversation as soon as she arrived.

Camila narrowed her eyes as she tried to remember the name of the girl who dared bring up the subject. Fernanda López, if she remembered right. The same one she'd seen hanging all over Carvalho earlier.

She took another sip of her drink before answering. "No deal. I just don't like people judging me without even knowing me."

"If you ask me, it looked more like a lot of sexual tension," López chimed in again.

She was quickly rising on Camila's shit list. At that rate, she would soon overtake Carvalho herself. At least the other girl had opted to avoid her since their incident.

"Well, nobody asked you."

She didn't care if she made another enemy. It was better to show López she shouldn't mess with her than have to deal with her stupid comments the whole season. López raised her hands in mock surrender.

"Does anyone know her?" Liz asked, probably trying to prevent her from making things worse by changing the subject. "I've never heard of her before, but she is so good. The way she scored today was like some Messi shit."

Camila suppressed a groan. Marveling at Carvalho's skills wasn't her idea of a fun time, but at least they'd moved on from her. She was curious too. As much as she hated Carvalho, Liz was right. The girl was good.

"You really need to pay attention to international teams," Stephanie Brown said. "She is probably one of the top players in the world right now, but she was on a small team in Brazil until Houston hired her."

When Brown spoke, people paid attention. It surprised Camila she was even here. The whole environment seemed so juvenile for someone of her caliber. A veteran US national team player mingling with a bunch of rookies. Maybe that was the point—to monitor them. She wasn't only a skilled player, but she had a reputation as a strategist. She knew everyone's strengths and weaknesses, and they couldn't have a better captain.

Camila tried to bite her tongue, but curiosity got the best of her. It was important to study the competition, she told herself. "You've seen her play?"

"I've had an eye on her since they called her to the Brazil national team for one of our friendlies. She only played for the last fifteen minutes, but she made us sweat during that time. When I looked her up, I couldn't believe she was only nineteen. I knew Antonia Carvalho would mean trouble for us in the future. I wasn't expecting to have her as a teammate, but it doesn't surprise me that an American team snatched her."

Camila wasn't sure when she stopped listening and started staring at Carvalho. The girl was standing across the pool with another group of players. She looked so different from how she had on the field. Her hair was down, flowing freely over her back, moving with the rhythm of her laughter. Her eyes, which had been full of anger when they played, now sparkled under the neon lights. She seemed taller too. Though she was still shorter than any of them, her shoulders stood straight, while on the field she seemed to have a weight pushing them down and curving her back.

Out of nowhere, a ball landed on Carvalho's chest, and she didn't miss a beat. She dominated it with ease, hitting it back and forth with the other players.

It was impossible for Camila to hear what was being said on the other side of the pool. Even if she could, she didn't know if it would help her understand why the Brazilian player was suddenly undressing. She controlled the ball, hit it back to someone else, and while they passed it around, she took off her shirt just in time to receive a pass. The same thing happened with her shoes and then her jeans.

For no apparent reason, the other girl now stood half-naked in front of everyone. Nobody seemed to mind, and Camila didn't care, of course. She was used to seeing women parading around with almost no clothes. It came with the territory of sharing a locker room. That same morning, she'd seen Carvalho changing, but it felt different to see it happen in plain view.

Once she was down to her underwear, the ball returned to her feet right on cue; she showed off her skills for a couple of minutes, then threw the ball over the pool and jumped to hit a scissor kick before falling into the water. So that's why she had to undress. Camila still didn't get what the point was, but at least there was some kind of explanation for the weird behavior.

She was so immersed in following Carvalho's movements that it took her by surprise when someone grabbed her arm and pulled her up. Before she could react, she was being dragged toward the pool. Around her, everyone was taking their clothes off and jumping in. She stood on the edge, watching her teammates laugh and splash around until she was the only one left high and dry. With a sigh, she removed her shirt and then her pants. She was almost done when the feeling of being watched made her scan the pool, only to see Antonia Carvalho staring back at her.

She expected the other girl to avert her eyes after being caught, but the Brazilian seemed to thrive on confrontation. She held her gaze steady, only moving her eyes away to travel the length of Camila's body, from head to toe and back until their eyes met again. Her gaze never wavered, almost as if challenging Camila to say something. She didn't. One fight in a day was enough. Instead, she strolled the length of the pool while looking for the ladder, then she lowered herself slowly into the water, feeling a pair of eyes burning her back the entire time. She wanted to show off a little. She knew she had a great body, and she couldn't think of a better way to spite the other girl than showing her what she would never have.

Antonia still didn't feel at ease with her teammates. Most of them seemed nice enough. Occasionally, she didn't understand what they were saying, but at least they seemed welcoming and warm. In a country where she knew no one, their company was all she had. They would never replace her brother, but they were a better option than an empty hotel room. The pool almost made her feel like she was back in Brazil. She preferred the beach, but if she closed her eyes, the sticky heat felt almost the same.

She floated around with her eyes closed, the loud blabbering of her teammates almost fading away. When she opened her eyes, her gaze landed on Sánchez, who was getting ready to join them in the water. She wasn't sure what exactly drew her to Sánchez when the team was full of attractive women, but when she undressed, Antonia couldn't tear her eyes away.

Her stare lingered on the smooth curves, and she marveled at the muscles in Camila's legs and arms.

Sánchez had a great body and an even prettier face; it was a shame she was so stuck-up. Life was too hard to spend it angry with the world, especially when you had no reason to be.

As Sánchez lowered herself into the water, Antonia forced herself to look away. No need to give the already arrogant woman more reasons to feel full of herself, and the last thing Antonia wanted was a repeat of their locker room confrontation.

"Anyone want to race?" she blurted out. When everyone stopped talking and looked at her, she elaborated. "Piggyback racing across the pool. The losing team takes a shot."

"Sounds fun!" López said. "We're a team," she added, yanking Antonia closer.

Antonia didn't hesitate to sit on López's shoulders. "Woo-hoo! Who's racing us?" she screamed.

"I'm game," Sánchez said from behind Antonia, with an edge to her voice she couldn't decipher. It sounded like a mix of annoyance and determination.

Antonia turned around with a smirk and a raised eyebrow, only to be met with a fierce scowl. That only made her smile wider.

Antonia let her eyes roam freely over Sánchez's body once again, fascinated by the way Sánchez pulled a blushing Young along with her and easily lifted the other girl on her shoulders. Young wasn't small by any means. Smaller than Sánchez, yes, but not small.

As soon as the race started, Antonia's competitiveness came out, and even more so when they fell behind. There was not much she could do from her position except wave her arms around and try to distract the other team. She splashed water in their direction and yelled at López to hurry, but it was useless.

She jumped down from López's shoulders and into the water.

"You're so slow. I'll carry you for the next race," Antonia said, smiling and bumping López softly with her hips.

López bumped back. "How about no. I'm like double your size. Would you be able to lift me up?"

"I'm stronger than I look." Antonia lowered her tone of voice. "I can show you any time."

López grinned. "Shut up."

"Time to pay up," Young said, interrupting their conversation and handing López a shot of tequila.

Another shot appeared in Antonia's line of vision. Sánchez moved the glass and lime directly in front of her eyes as if taunting her.

"Drink up," she said.

The icy stare she'd seen in Sánchez's eyes on the pitch had melted away, at least to a degree. It was hard to read the swirl of emotions in those hazel eyes, but Antonia swore it looked like she was enjoying herself. Whatever the reason, Antonia never backed down from a challenge.

Without breaking eye contact, she grabbed the shot and passed the tip of her tongue along the salt-rimmed border of the glass before gulping the amber liquid in one movement. When Sánchez was the first to look away after she'd licked her lips, Antonia smirked. Just because Sánchez was unbearable didn't mean she couldn't have fun with her. Her stuck-up attitude made it even more satisfying.

She was happy with her idea of racing. Everybody was having fun, but she didn't count on López being so freaking slow. They lost every single time, and after five tequila shots, Antonia wasn't feeling great.

"I'm out. I can't handle more tequila, and López is a lousy partner."

"Hey! I am, but you don't have to call me out like that," López yelled.

They got out of the water together and lay down on one of the pool chairs. López was as drunk as she was, maybe more. She crawled over Antonia and put her head on her chest.

"You're gonna be my best friend on this team. I've decided on it! No take-backs." López pinched Antonia's cheeks. "Say you will be my friend. Say it."

Antonia pushed her hand away. "That's fine by me, López. You're officially my best friend on the team."

"Yay!" López exclaimed, falling on top of Antonia to hug her.

Antonia felt someone watching them, but she didn't bother looking around this time. She already knew who it was. It was ironic that the person who had snapped at her for staring was now the same one who couldn't tear her eyes away from her.

"This party is dying down. We should go clubbing!" López exclaimed.

Antonia laughed. "Easy there, party girl. We have training tomorrow. We probably should get going."

She put her hand around López's waist and supported her as they walked to the last group of girls left to say goodbye—Jones, Sánchez, Young, O'Donnell, and a couple more.

"Thank you for the party, Jones," Antonia said.

"No problem." Jones gave López a once-over, watching as she struggled to stay upright even with Antonia holding her. "Are you guys okay getting home on your own?"

Antonia didn't hesitate to take the opening. She had no clue how to get home. She'd been in Houston barely a week, and the thought of navigating the city on her own to take López home terrified her. "No, actually.

López here was my ride, but she's in no state to drive. Could you help me call a cab or Uber?"

Jones got her phone out. "Where are you going?"

"I'm staying at a hotel downtown while the team finds me an apartment. López said something about being close to Rice?" Antonia subtly nudged López, hoping she was at least sober enough to give them the address.

"What? Oh . . . yeah, I'm like two blocks from Rice."

"Camila's place is also downtown. She can drive you," Young jumped in with more enthusiasm than the situation deserved. "And I'll take care of López. We live pretty close."

Sánchez didn't say a word, but her jaw clenched. Being volunteered to handle a drunk was probably the last thing she wanted.

"Thank you," Antonia said. "I'm fine with an Uber, but I would appreciate it if you made sure López gets home."

"Nonsense! Camila is driving that way. She'll take you," Young insisted, oblivious to the expression on Sánchez's face.

Antonia was about to reject the offer again when Sánchez spoke up for the first time. "Yeah, sure. I'll drive you," she said. Sánchez sounded as though she tried to make it sound casual, like she couldn't care less, but the tightness of her jaw betrayed her.

It was obvious, at least to Antonia, that she would rather do anything else in the world, but she couldn't get out of it without looking like an inconsiderate jerk. Maybe later, when nobody was paying attention, she would ditch Sánchez. For now, Antonia would take the offer. It was a fifteen-minute ride. What was the worst that could happen?

Chapter Four

Antonia helped López get into Young's car—a harder task than she'd imagined when she first offered, since López insisted on telling Young how beautiful she was and tried to climb onto her lap from the passenger's seat. In the end, the only way to get her to stay quiet long enough for Antonia to secure her seat belt was for Young to promise she'd let her spend the night at her place.

She made a mental note to tease the hell out of López the next day as she watched them drive away. The entire time, Sánchez stood next to them with one hand on her waist and the other dangling the keys. As soon as they left, she got in her own car and threw an exasperated look in Antonia's direction when she didn't move to join her right away.

Antonia clenched her jaw but rushed to get in the car. The sooner they started driving, the sooner she would be home and the less likely they'd fight again. There was not much of a view from the highway, but Antonia stared out the window anyway. Her only other option was to look at Sánchez, but she didn't want to test her luck no matter how sexy she found the permanent scowl that had taken over her face or the way her still-wet hair clung to her neck.

Antonia forced herself to remain quiet. She didn't want to have to figure out how to get to her hotel on her own, and she wouldn't put it past Sánchez to abandon her in the middle of the highway. It turned out that Sánchez was the one who couldn't go fifteen minutes without listening to the sound of her own voice.

"Do you make it a habit of getting drunk right before training and matches?" she said, her tone sharp and accusatory.

"Only on special occasions." She didn't know what Sánchez's problem with her was, but she was getting on her nerves. "Don't worry. Even hungover, I can beat you," she said with a fake innocent smile that spread when she noticed how hard Sánchez gripped the steering wheel.

"It's easy to look better than other players if you never pass the ball. Soccer is a team sport, in case you didn't get the memo."

"I'm happy to pass the ball when I can trust my teammates to deliver."

Sánchez slammed on the brakes, propelling Antonia forward. When she recovered from the sudden movement, she saw the sardonic smile on Sánchez's face.

"This is your stop."

There was no reason for Antonia to stay in the car. She should be eager to leave, should have jumped out as soon as possible. Instead, she returned Sánchez's sneer with a smirk of her own.

"Has anyone ever told you that you'd be far more likable if you relaxed a little?" Antonia said.

As expected, Sánchez's face contorted in anger.

"If you lost that clenched jaw and the furrowed eyebrows, I think it would bring out your eyes," she added.

The plan was to mock Sánchez. To make her angry. But the mistake was looking into her hazel eyes. Suddenly, Antonia was no longer looking at the annoying teammate but at the attractive girl who first caught her eye in the locker room.

Antonia leaned forward. "I have to admit you look hot when angry, but I could do without the superiority complex," she murmured.

Sánchez scoffed. "Superiority complex? As if you're not full of yourself."

Antonia's eyes remained locked with Sánchez's, unwavering under the heat of her gaze. "I'm only full of myself because I have reason to be." She moved another inch closer until there was barely any space left between them.

Sánchez glanced at her lips and then back into her eyes. Antonia expected her to move away, to turn her head around and push her out of the car, but she didn't. Sánchez moved closer, her nostrils flared and her scowl intensified and her eyes . . . Her eyes didn't stop staring at Antonia's lips.

She realized then that there was no way she'd leave that car without either kissing or fighting Sánchez. She opted for kissing—it seemed like the less damaging choice. She moved slowly, like a hunter afraid to scare a wild animal. She cupped her face first, never breaking eye contact, giving Sánchez all the time in the world to slap the hell out of her if she wanted to, before bringing their mouths together.

Despite the anger radiating between them seconds before, Antonia kissed her softly, barely grazing Sánchez's lips with her own. When the other girl didn't push her away, she dared to go in for another touch, and another. Each was as slow and measured as the first, until Sánchez grabbed the back of her head and pulled her closer with force, pushing her tongue against Antonia's lips, until she couldn't help but open her mouth and let their tongues meet.

Why was she kissing Antonia Carvalho? Camila had no idea. She wasn't even sure how it happened. One minute they were arguing, and the next, Antonia was looking at her with so much intensity that she was unable to look away.

Once Antonia's plump lips took over hers, Camila could only surrender to their warmth. They were softer than any lips she'd kissed before, and skilled too. She kind of hated how good of a kisser Antonia was. The other girl moved with purpose and firmness, and Camila followed the pace she set. While Antonia's lips were on hers, she was happy to surrender, to stop thinking and let someone else take the lead. It was something she didn't know she craved.

If anyone asked later, she would deny it, but when Antonia moved away, Camila couldn't bear the thought of losing the contact, of not having her warm breath tickling her lips and her expert tongue setting the pace. She grabbed Antonia's face and held her in place, hoping that would be enough to make her intentions obvious. Thankfully, Antonia needed little encouragement to kiss her again.

She suppressed a moan when Antonia's hand started crawling up her side. There wouldn't have been anything more embarrassing than moaning into Antonia's mouth. As much as Camila was enjoying the kiss, she didn't want to give the cocky girl the satisfaction of realizing just how much.

A loud honk made them jump apart. Their eyes met for a thousandth of a second, and Camila prayed that her own pupils didn't give away her desire like Antonia's were. Antonia moved toward her again, but a string of continuous honks prevented anything more.

"Yeah, yeah. I'm moving!" Camila screamed while putting the car in drive.

She circled around the block to clear the hotel entrance before the guy in the car behind them had a fit. She avoided looking at Antonia, suddenly very aware of what they'd been doing. Her mind, empty minutes before and only capable of focusing on Antonia's lips, was now swirling in a frenzy of thoughts.

Why, of all the players on the team, had she ended up stuck with the one who got under her skin? And why did Antonia have to be so attractive and such a good kisser? It was probably a game to her. It had to be a way to destabilize Camila or be able to brag the next day about how she'd gotten to her. Nothing else made sense.

The click of the car lock opening broke the silence. "See you tomorrow at practice," Camila said, her voice sharp.

She tried to not look at Antonia at first, afraid her resolve would crumble if she peered into her eyes and saw that same raw want she'd seen before. But she couldn't help but sneak a glance in her direction, only to find Antonia's mouth curved into a half smile, slightly parted as if she wanted to say something. Part of Camila hoped she did.

When Antonia opened the car door and stepped out, Camila fought to push down the disappointment. She watched her walk away with the memory of their kiss still on her lips.

Chapter Five

IT DIDN'T SURPRISE CAMILA in the least when she was the first one in the locker room the next day. She'd been one of the few to not drink, and she'd also arrived earlier than expected. After hours of tossing and turning in bed, she ended up getting ready and driving to the stadium. It was a better use of her time than staying in her apartment doing nothing.

She'd replayed the kiss with Antonia in her mind over and over again, wondering why she'd let it happen when she had plenty of chances to turn away. Why the pull of Antonia's presence had been so strong that she'd melted when their lips touched, against her best judgment. She couldn't undo the kiss, but she wanted to at least forget it. That wouldn't happen while she was alone in her apartment. Maybe practicing would help.

JOHANA GAVEZ

On the way to the field, she passed Coach Medina's office. "Sánchez," he said, exasperated. Camila turned around, afraid she had upset him by arriving so early, but before she could say anything, he added, "This is going to blow up in our faces."

The explanation she was about to offer died on her lips. Instead, she moved closer to the office door and strained her neck as if that would help her hear better.

"Easy for you to say, Sánchez. You're a World Cup champion. You'd get a slap on the wrist if shit goes down. I don't know if I'd be so lucky."

With her heart hammering in her chest, Camila slowly walked away and then took off running until she reached the pitch. The person on the other end of the phone had to be her dad. She struggled to make sense of what it meant, but it didn't sound like anything good. A sinking feeling settled in her stomach.

In her shock, she didn't notice Coach Megan approaching until she stood next to her.

"Hey, isn't it a little early for you to be here?"

"Umm . . ." Camila blinked twice, her mouth hanging open. "I wanted to get some extra practice."

"I'm done setting everything up, so I can help you run some drills."

"I can't say no to that offer."

It wouldn't be enough to shake her uneasiness at what she'd heard, but a one-on-one practice with her childhood idol was a dream come true. If something was going to help her get out of her own head, it was that.

By the time her teammates showed up, she'd already practiced free kicks, definitions from the goal area, and headshots with the help of Coach Megan. She'd been patient but demanding, highlighting her strengths but also pointing out her errors and giving her advice. Once again, Camila found it unfair that Coach Megan was still only an assistant coach when she was obviously more than qualified to lead a team.

"Whatever team gets you as their head coach will be incredibly lucky," Camila blurted out.

The coach snorted. "If I ever get the chance, sure. You'd think things would be better now, but there are still only two female head coaches in the league." She put a hand on Camila's shoulder. "The national team had to fight for equal pay for years despite being World Cup champions, and team owners still think a male coach will know better. But thank you for the sentiment. I appreciate it."

Camila sighed. "Well, if someone is going to break the glass ceiling, it's you. It wouldn't be the first time."

"I'll keep trying, that's for sure." She gave Camila another pat on the back. "Go join your teammates."

Camila jogged away, turning around to give Coach Megan one last look and an encouraging smile halfway through. She noticed the team was scattered around the field, split out in pairs for the warm-up and made a beeline for Liz, who stood alone on the far left side of the field.

"You look good," she said to Liz. "I can't say the same for the rest of the team." She surveyed the field and found pale faces and deep bags under the eyes of everyone around her.

"The magic of a cold shower," Liz replied.

Camila's gaze landed on Antonia. She looked better than most. Antonia was laughing, with one arm wrapped around López, who winced.

"So, how did that go?" Liz asked, looking in the same direction.

"What do you mean? I drove and dropped her off. How else was it supposed to go?" she snapped.

"Okay . . ."

She immediately felt bad, knowing that Liz was just trying to make conversation. "How did it go for you? López was a mess."

"It was better than expected."

Camila frowned, not understanding the answer. When her eyes met Antonia's across the field, her scowl only deepened.

"God, how are you so perky after yesterday? I'm dying," López moaned.

Antonia smiled and shrugged. "I told you, the key is to drink plenty of water before bed."

"That's your secret? Water?"

Antonia laughed softly and put a hand on López's shoulder. "No, I have blessed Brazilian genes. But since you don't, that's the best I can offer you."

She showed how good she felt by doing a couple of jumps.

López wrinkled her nose. "Ugh, my head hurts from watching you."

"For your sake, let's hope Coach Medina goes easy on us today." Antonia surveyed the pitch; all her teammates looked awful, except for Sánchez, Young, and Brown, who, as far as she remembered, hadn't had much to drink. "For everyone's sakes."

He didn't go easy on them. Running, physical conditioning, drills—everything under the scorching Houston heat. It was a miracle nobody passed out.

Antonia had no problem with the physical demands. She may have been a step slower than usual, but not enough for the coach to notice. Her mind, however, was another story. There'd been one thing occupying it since the night before. One person, to be more precise.

She was still trying to decipher why Sánchez had turned from hot to cold in a second. For a glorious moment, there was nothing but passion between them. While they kissed, Antonia believed that maybe she'd been wrong about Sánchez. The way she grabbed her head and brought her closer and the way she melted under her touch seemed so distant from the girl who now stood in front of her with a scowl.

It was like their first training together but worse. The day before, it had seemed to be just natural competitiveness. Now it seemed personal. Sánchez barely looked at her, and when she did, she always had an angry expression on her face. Antonia was torn between confronting her and pretending nothing had happened.

"Okay, everyone! Let's finish practice with some passing drills. Sánchez and Carvalho together, López and Jones."

As Coach Medina continued pairing them off, Antonia glanced at Sánchez, who looked like someone had put a rotten egg under her nose. She bit her tongue, took a deep breath, and tried to act as if it didn't bother her. She wouldn't give Sánchez the satisfaction of knowing she was getting to her.

She was the utmost professional as they practiced passes together, but with every look avoided, every sign of indifference Sánchez showed toward her, the desire to force Sánchez to tell her what her problem was grew.

After the practice, Antonia showered and changed as fast as possible, determined to not let the other girl get away. When Sánchez walked out, she followed, catching up with her in the parking lot.

"Hey, wait up!" she called, closing the distance between them.

Sánchez put her bag in the back seat and looked at her while opening the driver's door.

"Would you mind giving me a ride today too?" Antonia asked, expecting Sánchez to say no.

"Why don't you ask López? You've been glued to her since yesterday."

"She has a thing."

"A thing?" Sánchez replied, raising an eyebrow.

"Yeah, a thing."

"Fine, but don't make this a habit. I'm not your personal driver." Sánchez got in and slammed the driver's door, but she waited for Antonia.

After minutes of silence on the road, Antonia tried her luck as they exited the highway. "You seemed upset during practice."

"I don't like when people slack off."

Antonia fought the urge to roll her eyes. There went any hopes she had of enjoying a nice, trivial conversation with Sánchez. "I don't think anybody was slacking off. They were just sick."

"Hungover, not sick. It was their choice."

"You were at the party too."

"I didn't get drunk because I know what responsibility means."

"I don't think anybody on the team wants to do badly," Antonia said. "We were having fun and things got a little out of hand, but it was a once-in-a-lifetime thing. It won't happen again. It didn't affect a competition, and we all enjoyed ourselves."

Sánchez scoffed. "I think it showed their character. I'm here to win, not to party. Unlike some people, I have goals."

"I'm sure everyone on the team has their own dreams and goals. Just because different people may have different ways of going about them doesn't mean they don't care." Before Sánchez could reply, Antonia decided to change the topic. It was obvious she wasn't getting anywhere with this line of questioning. "It seemed like you were angry at me more than anyone else."

For a long time, Sánchez didn't answer. She focused on the road; the scowl Antonia was now already familiar with took over her features. She was about to try another angle when Sánchez answered.

"You seem set on meddling in things that don't concern you, so I'm going to be honest with you. Maybe that way you'll stop asking." She looked at Antonia for a brief second before returning her eyes to the road. "I was more upset at you because even though it pains me to admit it, you're talented. Despite being just as hungover as anyone else, or more than, you played as great as always. It makes me angry when people who make no effort succeed anyway."

The gall of this girl.

Antonia took a deep breath. "You think I've made no effort?"

Sánchez shrugged, infuriating Antonia even more.

"You don't know what you're talking about. Life has thrown enough things my way that I don't need to look for stupid reasons to be upset. I choose to take every opportunity I get to enjoy myself instead." Her voice was clear and never betrayed her annoyance, but she couldn't help throwing a dig in Sánchez's direction. "Someone who has had everything handed to them in life wouldn't understand."

She knew Sánchez would hate to be called entitled again. Antonia may have only known her for a couple of days, but it was obviously a sore spot.

"You don't know a thing about my life," Sánchez retorted through gritted teeth.

"You know nothing about my life either, yet you insist on judging me and everyone around you. Have you ever heard the saying 'Don't do to others what you don't want people to do to you'?"

Sánchez didn't answer.

Antonia turned away and stared out the window. She was tired of being the only one trying to fix their relationship. They didn't need to be friends in order to play together. If that's what Sánchez wanted, then Antonia was fine with it.

Why did this girl get under her skin so easily? And why did she insist on talking to her when Camila wanted her as far away as possible? But no, of course she'd forced them to spend time together. Camila was still kicking herself for not being fast enough to come up with an excuse to not drive her home. It wouldn't happen again. From that moment on, she would make sure their only contact was in practice and during games.

Camila didn't see what was so wrong about her having a work ethic and hating when people did stupid things like get drunk when they knew they had practice the next day. She was committed and responsible, that was all. She'd worked as hard as anyone for her spot on the team, and she wasn't going to be all smiles and sunshine when the entire team might suffer because one of them wasn't taking things seriously.

She didn't care what stupid Antonia Carvalho thought of her, but she wouldn't allow anyone to call her entitled.

"You didn't seem to mind me having everything handed to me on a silver platter when you shoved your tongue down my throat yesterday."

She regretted the words as soon as they left her mouth. She'd spent the entire day trying to pretend the kiss never happened and wanted desperately to forget it had. And there she was, bringing it to light again. When Antonia sported the same half smile from the day before, Camila regretted it even more.

"What does that have to do with anything?"

There was something in Antonia's voice—a hint of glee, or maybe a bit of mockery—that got on Camila's nerves.

"I think you're mad because I didn't fall for your charming act, and that's why you're attacking me right now," Camila answered with as much confidence as she could muster.

"Hmm . . . If we call grabbing my head to not let me get away not falling for it, I guess you're right."

Now Camila was sure Antonia was making fun of her. The smirk taking over her face was all the evidence she needed.

"That was an instinctive reaction. Nothing to do with you."

"Sure, keep telling yourself that."

Camila clenched her teeth, infuriated at how Antonia was able to gain the upper hand in their conversation. It was her own fault for bringing the kiss up, but now she couldn't backtrack. The last thing she needed was to lose another verbal spar with Antonia.

"You're so full of yourself," she said. A weak retort, but it was the best she had.

"It's called confidence. If I kissed you again right now, I bet you would kiss me back."

Camila cursed internally at the fact that the mention of another kiss sent a rush of excitement through her body. "If you kissed me right now, we would die because we're in the middle of the highway," she said.

"Technically, that's true. But it's interesting how you didn't deny that you would enjoy it."

Camila wanted to erase the smug look from Antonia's face. "You're the most infuriating person I've ever met."

Antonia's smirk got bigger. "Not denying it again."

She glared at Antonia with all the anger she could channel toward her before focusing again on the road.

"I have an idea," Antonia said with an enthusiasm that scared Camila. "Come up to my room. If you can spend two hours without kissing me, you get whatever you want—me not speaking to you ever again, cleaning your apartment all year, paying for all your meals for a week. You name it."

"That's ridiculous. The last thing I want is to spend more time than necessary with you."

"I guess I win."

"You didn't win just because I refuse to take part in this stupid bet," Camila answered, voice raised. Antonia's stubborn attitude and cockiness was making her lose her cool.

"If you don't want to spend two hours with me, I can only assume it's because you know you can't resist me."

"There's nothing to resist because I don't like you," Camila said. This time, she spoke as slow as she could to get her point across.

"If you don't like me, then spending two hours without kissing me would be a piece of cake. What do you have to lose?"

"My valuable time."

"What are you doing after you drop me off that's so important?" Antonia insisted.

"Picking up dinner, watching TV. Some people enjoy their alone time."

She needed to learn to come up with better excuses. She already knew such a weak argument wouldn't deter Antonia.

"I'll cook and you can watch TV."

"Ugh. Fine, but we'll go to my apartment. If I have to deal with you, I at least want to be in my space."

The remainder of the ride was quiet the rest of the way. Camila guessed that Antonia's silence was probably because she didn't feel the need to keep bothering her after she'd achieved what she wanted. Camila's own silence was because the prospect of spending more time alone with Antonia filled her with dread. She hated Antonia. Her attitude, her confidence, and the way she constantly questioned her were infuriating, but the memory of their kiss the day before remained clear as day in her head. She would be lying if she didn't admit, at least to herself, that maybe she wouldn't hate kissing Antonia again.

If they didn't kiss but she had to deal with Antonia being annoying for two hours, she lost. If she gave in and kissed her, she lost too. She was sure she would never hear the end of it if she proved Antonia right. No matter what Camila did, the next two hours would be torture.

Chapter Six

CAMILA BRACED HERSELF FOR the awkwardness, but apparently, Antonia didn't know what shame meant. She made a beeline for the kitchen and opened the fridge as if they were the best of friends and she'd been in her apartment a hundred times. It was better than fumbling around, not knowing how to act around each other, but it bothered Camila to see how Antonia always seemed at ease when she herself had to struggle to fit in every single time. She didn't remember one time in her life when she didn't have to fight to be accepted. And here was Antonia, not caring about what she thought, making friends in one day, and acting as if she owned every place she walked into.

"There's not much to work with," Antonia said, staring in the freezer.

Camila dropped her duffel bag by the door and sat on the couch. "You're the one who offered to cook. I never said that was actually an option. I usually get takeout."

Antonia rummaged through the fridge, scooting things around, taking them out, and putting them back in again. "I could do something with the milk and cheese. Do you have pasta?"

"I think there's some instant mac and cheese in the cupboard."

"That will do."

Antonia got to work, navigating the kitchen with certainty. At first, Camila was determined to ignore her, to pretend her presence didn't faze her. She was going to watch TV and act as if Antonia wasn't there at all.

That plan lasted less than five minutes.

The sound of pans being moved, and Antonia mumbling under her breath in what Camila assumed was Portuguese, proved too much of a distraction. Camila fidgeted with her phone and sneaked glances at her from the living room until she finally sighed and moved to one of the stools next to the breakfast bar. Antonia glanced her way but resumed whisking without saying a word to her. Instead, she started singing. Camila didn't understand a word, and Antonia's voice wasn't showstopping by any means, but it mesmerized her. She stared at Antonia until her own self-consciousness made her break the silence between them.

"So, you like cooking?"

Antonia didn't look at her and remained focused on the task at hand. "Yeah, I guess." She tasted the sauce and gave an approving moan. "After my mom died, my brother and I would take turns cooking for each other. There was not much room to be creative when we only had rice, maybe eggs if we were lucky, and whatever the neighbors could give us. So, when I started earning some money and could afford to buy other stuff, I found it fun to be more creative. And with my brother working as a cook at a resort, he had plenty of ideas we could try together."

Camila opened her mouth but closed it again. She didn't know how to respond to the way Antonia had shared that tidbit of personal information as if it was not a big deal.

"What are you making?" she settled on saying. "That looks like a lot of effort for boxed mac and cheese."

"It's still boxed mac and cheese, but I'm making a carbonara sauce with the two slices of bacon you had left to give it a different taste."

"It smells good. My culinary abilities begin and end with instant meals."

"I can see that," Antonia replied with a small half smile.

Camila smiled back. To her surprise, the comment didn't upset her. For once she didn't think Antonia was judging her or trying to insult her. While the other girl focused on cooking, Camila observed her up close without fear of being called out.

Antonia was unaware—or pretended to be, for her sake—of the way Camila's eyes traveled the length of her body and traced the soft curves of her face. A curl had fallen out of the tight ponytail Antonia wore for training, and Camila became mesmerized as she watched it bounce, almost dance, as Antonia moved. She could have stayed lost on the plump lips that brought back memories from the night before, or the thick eyebrows that seemed to always be questioning her—if not for the fact that Antonia chose to look up at her then. The intensity in her eyes was too much for Camila to handle. It was one thing to stare inadvertently at Antonia; it was another to be confronted with her beauty and her teasing smirk up close.

To escape the pull Antonia had over her, Camila busied herself with setting the table and pouring their drinks. Antonia served two plates of pasta, which included sprinkled paprika and chopped basil Camila didn't even remember she had in the fridge.

"Enjoy," Antonia said, putting the plate on the table with perfect serving form.

Camila didn't eat at first, distracted by the joy emanating from Antonia at her accomplishment and the enthusiastic way she shoved food into her mouth. She accentuated each bite with a soft hum.

"This is fantastic," Antonia said. "I know I'm biased, but it is."

Camila took a bite of her own. "It's great. Makes me almost not regret letting you stay."

Antonia smirked. "I'll take that as a win."

That smirk again, teasing and provocative. Camila wasn't sure if it came naturally to Antonia, or if she was using it on purpose to throw her off her game. She couldn't get herself to ask. She could only look away to prevent being pulled in by it.

After dinner, they settled on the couch to watch TV. The couch was big enough that Camila could put space between them without being too obvious about the discomfort it caused her to have Antonia too close. She was determined to not let Antonia win the stupid bet, even if she'd never wanted the bet to happen in the first place and she wasn't even sure she'd agreed to it.

It turned out that waiting out the two hours wasn't even that hard. She wasn't sure what she had expected, but it wasn't for Antonia to act as if they were two friends hanging out instead of teasing her or trying to break her somehow.

"Two hours," Antonia said, looking at her watch. "You win."

What was the point of making up the ridiculous bet, bothering her until she accepted, and then doing nothing to win it? She didn't want Antonia. The last thing she needed was a repeat of their kiss, but Antonia's indifference felt like an insult. It was like she wanted to prove how easy it was for her to not care about Camila. To rub the fact that their kiss meant nothing to her in Camila's face.

Antonia looked at her with a soft smile. Camila hated that evidence of Antonia's mockery. Of her apathy. She was going to erase that smile from her face before she left. She wouldn't let her get away with proving whatever point it was she was trying to prove. There was only one way to get back at Antonia, and it was to beat her at her own game.

Camila climbed on the couch and crawled toward Antonia until she hovered over her. It was her turn to smirk when she saw the surprise in Antonia's eyes and the way she glanced at her lips. She pushed their mouths together in a sloppy kiss and moved even closer, letting the weight of her body rest on top of Antonia. To her satisfaction, Antonia grabbed her ass and pulled her down even closer as they kissed.

Camila slid her hand under Antonia's shirt and traced the curve of her waist. Every time a flick of Antonia's tongue made her lose the tiny amount of control she had left, she grasped at rock-hard abs to center herself again. Soon Camila grew more adventurous, moving her hands up and down the exposed skin, gripping and grabbing without restraint.

Antonia frantically kissed her back and slowly but surely shifted their bodies, trying to reverse their positions. Camila considered resisting the move, for no other reason than to not let Antonia win and take the lead, but the delicious movements of Antonia's tongue inside her mouth distracted her too much to focus on stopping her. All desire to do so vanished the moment Antonia climbed on top and pressed her entire body flush against hers.

She missed Antonia's mouth as soon as she moved it away, but Camila forgot about chasing it down when Antonia latched on to her neck moments later, sucking and nipping directly at one of her most sensitive areas. When Antonia got up, pulling Camila up with her, she followed without hesitation. They never stopped kissing as they walked to the bedroom. Antonia led her there, moving around the apartment with the same confidence she'd showed only an hour before in the kitchen. As if she owned the place. This time Camila didn't mind. She didn't want to think or stop to point her in the right direction. She only wanted to feel, to lose herself in the passion of Antonia's kisses and not worry about anything else.

The foot of the bed hitting her legs served as the only warning she got before falling on top of the mattress, with Antonia following behind with a lot more grace. Antonia lowered herself on top of her, hands guarding Camila's face and her petite body hovering over Camila but not fully lying on her.

For the first time since they started devouring each other, they stared into each other's eyes. If there was any chance of them stopping, of avoiding what was about to happen, it was then. Camila wouldn't be able to pretend there was no opportunity to stop what they were doing before it got out of hand, because right then, in that instant, they asked each other for permission with one look. When her eyes met the deep brown ones above her, she saw more than lust swirling in the dark pupils.

Antonia held her gaze, unwavering, immobile, as if waiting for Camila to give her a sign. There was raw passion in her eyes, but also a small sliver of . . . care? The softness made the breath catch in Camila's throat. Her gaze dropped to Antonia's lips, in part to avoid those eyes, and in part because she missed them. She pushed the bit of hesitation to the back of her mind. She wanted more.

Camila nodded. As if on cue, Antonia claimed her lips again for what felt like too short of a time. She then moved down to leave a trail of kisses on any vestige of exposed skin. With her eyes closed, Camila savored the warm, wet touches on her neck and collarbone while her skin erupted in goose bumps in every spot Antonia kissed.

The sound of her own ragged breaths and the soft whimper that came out of her lips broke the spell. Camila realized how in control Antonia seemed while she herself writhed under her and made it obvious how much of an effect she had. It scared her how desperately she wanted Antonia in that moment. It was one thing to want her, and another to let her see it so easily, so plainly.

Without a word, she pushed Antonia away, removed her shirt, and took off her own. When Antonia tried to restart their kissing, Camila turned, instead rolling Antonia onto her back and climbing on top of her. There was a pang of something that felt a lot like longing at the loss of Antonia's body on top of hers, but taking control was more important in that moment. Allowing herself to surrender to Antonia, no matter how much she ached for it, would be too much, too fast.

Antonia didn't fight her. She seemed equally at ease following as she was leading. Once their shirts were off, Camila didn't see a reason to delay what they both wanted. She stood up and undressed almost entirely, leaving only her boxers on. Antonia followed her cue, squirming to take all her clothes off while lying in bed.

Camila gave herself a moment to enjoy the view—fully this time. Yes, she'd sneaked glances here and there, but now she could stare freely. She drank in every inch of Antonia's body, from the lean legs to the brown skin that glistened with sweat and invited her to lick every drop.

She ran her tongue across Antonia's firm stomach first, then up her sides to her neck and down again to her small breasts. Every shiver from Antonia, every sound, every hitched breath encouraged her to keep going. Not that she needed much encouragement. She was already addicted to the taste of Antonia's skin. Addicted to the sound of her gasps, to the muffled whimpers Antonia let out when Camila sucked a spot right above her left breast.

She enjoyed the way it was now, with Antonia squirming under her, pushing her hips forward as if she wanted their cores to meld together. She could have stayed just like that, devouring that neck and licking that soft skin, but a sense of urgency overcame her. Her senses were so focused on Antonia—her smell, her touch, her noises—that everything else felt like a blur. Like a dream she would wake up from at any minute. She wanted to enjoy as much as she could before the moment ended.

Staring directly into those brown eyes, Camila moved her hand down and slid it inside Antonia's underwear to caress the nub that waited for her in a pool of wetness. The moment the tip of her finger made contact, Antonia's eyes closed, and her mouth parted in an almost silent exclamation that sent shivers through Camila's body.

She regretted leaving Antonia's underwear on, but even when the tight fabric limited her movements, she didn't dare stop to take the underwear off, even if for only seconds. She became intoxicated by the effect that her soft, slow movements had on Antonia, and she didn't want to stop looking at the expressions on her face as she touched her.

She kept going, drinking in every sound and reaction, mesmerized by the drops of sweat that slid down Antonia's neck and tempted her to lean down to lick them. As she ran her tongue over Antonia's tender skin, Camila realized there was nothing stopping her from doing what she wanted. She licked and nipped and bit, always making sure to not lose the cadence with her hand.

They were so close that the air escaping Antonia's mouth with every moan hit Camila's ear, tickling it and making her form a moan of her own in her throat. She tried to suppress it and stop it from coming out, but it was a losing battle. The only way she found to disguise it amid her desperation was by biting Antonia's neck. She tried to control the strength of the bite, but the moment Antonia responded to the graze of her teeth with the loudest, most desperate sound she'd made so far, Camila couldn't stop herself from biting harder.

The way Antonia clutched at the sheets and bent over at her touch was mesmerizing. Camila had her literally at her fingertips, while the rest of the time it was always Antonia who had the upper hand and knew how to get under Camila's skin. The sense of power and control increased her pleasure even without being touched. She'd never experienced that before, and she had no plan to let go of that feeling. She wanted to enjoy it as long as she could, but the moment ended way too soon for her liking when Antonia's body went limp under her with one last silent moan.

Camila was not sure how long it was before Antonia recovered and started moving under her again. It was probably only a couple of minutes, but it felt like hours. The moment Antonia had come undone, Camila didn't know what to do, what would happen next. She didn't want to stop. She needed more of Antonia. The taste she had was not enough to satiate her.

Antonia seemed as eager as she was to continue their night together. Before Camila could react, Antonia used the weight of her body to flip her over, reversing their positions. She moved down, distracting Camila with wet kisses planted on the curve of her waist, her stomach, and the start of her pelvis as she rode her boxers down, kissing every inch of newly exposed skin, and then her own underwear. For the first time, they were fully exposed to each other, and the only thing Camila could think about when her eyes fell on Antonia's perfect center, glistening with wetness, was how much she wanted to touch, kiss, and drink it in, and to be touched and kissed in return.

She launched herself up again to capture Antonia's lips. As they kissed, she tried to change their positions again, but Antonia didn't allow it. A firm hand on her chest kept Camila in place.

"It's my turn," Antonia said between hungry kisses.

Camila tried to flip them again. "I never said I was done."

Antonia grinned and leaned down to bite the tip of her earlobe before whispering, "I'm sure we can find a way for both of us to get what we want."

Before Camila could react, Antonia moved away. She wasn't happy about the interruption. Even one second without tasting her was too long, but when Antonia sat with her legs spread, Camila's annoyance gave way to confusion.

Antonia patted the space between her legs. "Come here."

Camila obeyed, still not sure what Antonia had in mind but eager to do anything that brought her closer to enjoying her body again. She raised her eyebrows at Antonia while sliding into position. Antonia didn't answer her silent question. Instead, she moved closer, almost as if she wanted to straddle her but without fully lying on top of her. Their cores almost touched as their legs intertwined.

Camila didn't feel sexy at all. It was awkward, and the height she had on Antonia forced her to bend her back, making her uncomfortable. She gave Antonia the benefit of the doubt, but in the back of her mind, she wondered if she was messing with her. She wouldn't put it past her to try a prank in the middle of sex.

As soon as their bodies aligned, she realized there was no prank. Antonia grabbed Camila's hand and moved it only inches away from where she wanted it, while sliding two fingers inside Camila at the same time. Camila lost her focus for a few seconds. The fullness of the fingers, along with the subtle pressure of Antonia's palm on her mound, sent a rush of pleasure to her stomach.

When Antonia didn't move her hand, Camila almost snapped at her, until she realized why she was doing it. She was simply giving Camila time to mimic her actions. Antonia clearly wanted both of them to please each other at the same time. It was the only reason for their position to make sense, and Camila was happy to oblige. She wanted to feel Antonia inside her more than anything, except maybe getting to feel Antonia wrapped around her own fingers.

She used two fingers, just as Antonia had done, and was rewarded immediately by a mirrored movement inside her. It was hard to focus on the motions of her own hand when the tension inside of her kept building. She stopped several times without realizing, only starting again when soft encouragement from Antonia reminded her.

She forced herself to focus, to push down the waves of pleasure coming from her core and expanding over her entire body. She wanted to make sure Antonia enjoyed herself, but she also didn't want to let Antonia take the upper hand in their encounter. She wanted to watch Antonia come undone more than anything else.

The sight of Antonia gripping the sheets with one hand and the way she failed at reciprocating her movements like Camila had at the beginning only served as more motivation. She knew that if she kept going, she would soon be rewarded with what she most desired. She maintained the same rhythm and pressure until Antonia bent her back in pleasure. Then, and only then, did she allow herself to let go.

Sweaty and exhausted, they crawled up in the bed to lie down, side by side. They didn't hold each other, and although almost imperceptible, a purposeful gap separated them. The smell of sex in the air made Camila glance down to sneak a look at Antonia's glistening center. She wanted to taste her, to inhale her essence. Instead, she bit her lip and stared up at the ceiling.

She threw a sheet over their naked bodies and turned around, away from Antonia. She wouldn't toss her out, but she didn't want to leave any space for misunderstandings. There could be nothing more than sex between them. She still couldn't stand Antonia's cockiness.

"I still hate you," she said, half-asleep.

"That's fine. I still hate you too," Antonia replied.

Antonia was almost done cooking breakfast when Sánchez walked out of the bedroom. She glanced at her for only a second before focusing on the stove again, but that second was enough to catch the confused expression on Sánchez's face. Antonia fought to suppress a smile. Of course Sánchez would have expected to wake up and find her gone. She wasn't sorry to disappoint her. Even if she left, they would run into each other at practice in a couple of hours, so she didn't see the point.

"Right on time. Breakfast is ready," Antonia said.

"Yeah, I think the smell of food woke me up. Thanks," Sánchez replied, sitting down at the kitchen bar.

Antonia smiled and put an omelet in front of her. She could feel the tension radiating from Sánchez's body, but she stayed quiet. She was curious to see how long Sánchez could go without bringing up their night together or throwing her out of her place.

"Coffee? Or I also made vitamina de abacate. It's like an avocado smoothie. I love it."

Camila scrunched up her nose in the most adorable way. "Avocado smoothie? I'll stick to the coffee, please. More milk than coffee, and a lot of sugar."

After serving Sánchez her coffee, Antonia sat next to her. The sounds of cutlery and chewing were the only ones as they ate. Sánchez glanced her way several times, but Antonia did her best to pretend she didn't notice.

"You showered?" Sánchez asked.

Antonia stopped eating and tucked a stray piece of wet hair behind her ear. "Yeah, I woke up early. I hope you don't mind."

"No, no. It's fine," Sánchez rushed to say. "Do you need me to drive you home before practice?"

Antonia suppressed a smile again at the subtle attempt at getting her out of the apartment. She debated between making Sánchez suffer a little more or clearing the air once and for all. She opted for the latter to not risk a fight that would affect them on the pitch.

"I can get an Uber, don't worry." She watched the way Sánchez's shoulders relaxed at the possibility of her leaving, but her devious side wouldn't allow her to let the opportunity to mess with Sánchez slide. "But I was thinking we could drive to practice together."

As expected, Sánchez's eyes opened bigger than the sunny-side up eggs they were eating.

"What?"

"I have a change of clothes in my bag, so I don't really need to go to my hotel, and we only have an hour left before practice. I have no problem waiting so we can ride together."

Sánchez said nothing back and just stared at her with wide eyes.

Antonia shrugged. "Look, we're both adults here, right? I've never understood when people sneak out after a one-night stand. It was fun. I know you want nothing else from me, and I want nothing else from you. But we still have to see each other every day, and we play on the same team. There's no need for awkwardness."

At those words, Sánchez seemed to react—at least, the mask of coolness slipped back into place. "I don't have a problem driving you since you're already here, but we're not friends, so don't make it a habit."

Antonia grinned. She didn't believe for one second that this would be the only time they ended up in bed together. But she was not one to push people, at least not on that topic, so she would let Sánchez believe what she wanted.

"Sure. We're not friends. Super clear on that, Sánchez, don't worry."

Sánchez pushed her half-eaten breakfast away. "I better get ready. We don't want to be late," she said, walking back to her room.

Chapter Seven

"You should stop staring," López said in a plain, matter-of-fact tone. There wasn't any judgment in her voice.

Antonia averted her gaze from Sánchez. "I'm not staring." It was an obvious, ridiculous lie she expected López to rightfully call out.

"We've all been there, my friend." López used Antonia's shoulder as support while she stretched her legs.

"Been where?" Antonia glanced at Sánchez for less than a second.

"Pining for a stuck-up, sometimes straight girl."

"She is not straight, and I'm not pining."

"I'll concede the first point. And if it's any consolation, as much as you stare at her, she looks at you even more. The stuck-up part, though. Not even up for discussion."

"I just don't get her," Antonia muttered, more talking to herself than to López. Even after spending the night together, she didn't know where she stood with Sánchez. Worst of all, she wasn't sure why she cared.

"What's there to get?"

"I don't know. Why does she seem to hate me?"

"Jealousy?" López shot back, dropping the leg she was holding up and switching to stretch the other. "Why does it matter?"

Antonia didn't have an answer, so instead of offering one, she deflected. "What about you? How's that crush on Young working out?"

López glared at her. "I don't know what you're talking about."

"Oh?" Antonia snickered. "Did you forget how you were all over the poor woman after the party?"

López yanked her leg up, causing Antonia to almost lose her balance. "Your turn to stretch."

Antonia laughed and reached forward with her hands to touch the tips of her toes as López held her leg up. "Injuring me won't get you out of answering."

"I wish I'd forgotten how I made a fool of myself in front of her." She sighed. "I can never look at her again. I would die of embarrassment."

"It wasn't that bad," Antonia said, trying to cheer López up once she realized how mortified she was. "And you were drunk. I'm sure she won't hold it against you."

"We really are a pair, aren't we? I embarrass myself in front of the cutest girl on the team, and you pick a fight with your crush less than a minute after knowing her."

Antonia glanced at Sánchez in the distance once more. She wouldn't call it a crush per se, but there was attraction. If Sánchez wasn't so set on pushing her away, who knew what could happen.

"Yeah, we really are quite the pair."

Coach Medina called the entire team to the middle of the pitch with a potent scream halfway through the practice. A deep frown lined his face, but Antonia didn't care if he was about to rip them to pieces since it gave her a chance to grab one of the cold bottles of water waiting for them. She drank half and doused the other half over her head. Houston's heat was like nothing Antonia had ever experienced—not even in the hottest days in Florianópolis—but she pushed through.

"This Sunday, we'll have our first match as a team," he said with his usual gruff voice. "I don't want you to think that because it's only a friendly game, I expect less than excellence from any of you."

"Yes, Coach," they answered in unison.

"This match will give me a better idea of the lineup I can use in the upcoming tournament, so today we're going to split into two teams to see what combination of players works best. Nothing is final yet."

Coach Medina never said which was the potential starter team, but it wasn't hard to deduce. When Antonia was called to join the team that had Stephanie Brown as captain, she knew she had to be one of the starters. There was no way any coach would put a United States national team star on the bench.

She wasn't the only one to realize the obvious. The coach sent Sánchez to the opposing team, and she didn't seem happy. Their eyes met across the pitch, but there was only coldness and anger looking back at her. Any vestige of friendliness from early that morning was gone. Nobody enjoyed being on the bench, but losing your spot to someone you'd slept with the night before had to sting even more.

Antonia tried to put herself in Sánchez's shoes. They had the same dream, and of course, being put on the second team would suck. Why was that anger directed at her and not the coach or anyone else, though? That was harder for Antonia to understand. Maybe she was an easier target. It was a shame. She had fun with Sánchez, but she didn't want to deal with her bad temper, and she had a feeling that's what she would find if she tried to approach her. Staying away and focusing on playing was the best choice.

That was easier said than done.

They kept butting heads on the pitch. There was almost no reason for them to cross paths as often as they did, but somehow she ran into Sánchez more than she did the other team's defenders. That wasn't a problem in itself, except for the fact that Sánchez was playing rougher than a practice game warranted. Antonia tried to bite her tongue, control her temper, let things slide. But eventually, there was one push too many.

She was running down the left band, ready to throw a long pass, when something collided against her back and sent her flying to the ground. Antonia had always hated that about her smaller size, how it made it easier for other players to bump her, but she'd learned to be fast enough to avoid it. They couldn't hit you if they couldn't catch you.

As soon as she hit the grass, she knew who'd bumped into her even without having to look up. She sprung back up and made a beeline toward Sánchez.

"What's your problem?" she said, getting in her face.

Sánchez moved even closer, breathing heavy. "You're my problem."

The rest of the team jumped to intervene. Antonia felt a hand on her chest, pushing her backward. Young tried to pull Sánchez away with little success. It wasn't until Coach Medina got there that they both stepped back.

"Hey, that's enough. Both of you, go to the locker room."

"What!" Sánchez exclaimed.

Antonia gritted her teeth. If someone should be upset at being sent away, it should be her. She was only answering Sánchez's attacks, but she knew Coach Medina wouldn't care. There was no point arguing.

"Count yourself lucky I'm not suspending you from practice for a week. I don't care what your problem with each other is. We're a team. While you're playing on the same field, you leave your issues outside. Now go, before I change my mind and think of a better punishment for your childishness."

Antonia nodded and walked away without protest. Sánchez huffed behind her—at least she wasn't stupid enough to go against the coach. The last thing Antonia wanted was to be trapped in a confined space with Sánchez, but there was no way around it. At least half an hour remained before practice ended, and she knew the coach would want to talk to them. They had to wait.

At least their lockers were at opposite ends of the locker room. She knew the chances of Sánchez talking to her were slim, but Antonia still slipped her earbuds. The faint sound of music wasn't enough to mask the sound of Sánchez throwing her boots against the metal chair.

"I hope you're freaking happy."

Antonia wanted to ignore her. She tried her best, but as soon as the words reached her ears, she had to reply. She wouldn't take the blame for something that wasn't her fault.

She stood up and took her earbuds out. "Are you for real? You're the one who pushed and faulted me the whole practice."

"I was playing. Doing my job. It's not my fault if you can't take a little rough play."

"Oh please, drop the act. Nobody buys it. You know I can take some rough play; I showed you last night." She knew it was a low blow to bring up their encounter the night before, but she was angry and no longer cared. "I don't know why you're back to being an annoying brat."

Sánchez walked in her direction. They were inches apart again, and this time there was nobody to separate them. "There it is. I knew it," she said, pushing a finger into Antonia's chest. "You used me. Distracted me with the stupid party and with last night so you could take my spot on the starting team."

Antonia couldn't help but laugh. "That makes no sense. How could having sex last night influence the coach's choices?"

She waited for an answer that never came. Of course, even Sánchez had to see how stupid her reasoning was, but she still didn't back down. That made the most vicious side of Antonia come out. She could be nice and fun, but she didn't stand back when people attacked her. And Sánchez was about to find that out the hard way.

"I had recruiters traveling to Brazil to beg me to join this team," Antonia said. "My agent has half a dozen offers for me if I decide to go somewhere else. I don't need to sabotage anyone to get a spot. It's not my fault you're used to Daddy making everything easy for you and that you can't handle rejection. If you want to know why you're not on the starter team, maybe look at yourself instead of blaming other people."

She was spared from a response when Jones came into the locker room to tell them the coach wanted to see them in his office. Antonia shared one last glare with Sánchez before walking away.

She was ready for the worst once they reached Coach Medina's office—being suspended, even fired from the team.

"I don't want explanations. I don't want excuses," he said. "What happened today can't ever happen again." He paused and looked at them for their reaction. When they nodded, he resumed speaking. "I'm here to make this team a winner, and I can't do that if my players are fighting. We have a match this weekend in San Diego, and I've instructed management that you two will share a room." He held his hand up to stop their protests as soon as they started. "I don't need you to be best friends, only to be cordial. One more fight, one more incident, and you're both off the team. Understood?"

"Yes, sir."

Chapter Eight

CAMILA'S PLAN IN SAN Diego was to stay away from Antonia. Just because their coach had forced them to room together didn't mean she couldn't avoid Antonia as much as possible the rest of the time—at practice, on the team bus, on the flight. If she was lucky, by the time she made it to the room, the other girl would be fast asleep and they wouldn't even need to talk.

After the heat of the moment had worn off, Camila realized she'd been out of line. Antonia was right that she was directing her resentment over not being on the starter team at the wrong person. She was angry at herself for failing, but it was easier to blame Antonia. She would never admit that to the presumptuous Brazilian, though. Even if she'd been wrong, Antonia had no right to insult her in response.

At least she had Liz on her side. She allowed Camila to hide in the room she shared with López.

"You know you can't stay here forever, right?" Liz said. She stopped typing on her phone to raise an eyebrow in Camila's direction.

"I don't see why not. We should just switch. I'm sure López would be happy to sleep in the same room with Antonia. They're on top of each other all the time as it is."

"They're just friends," Liz replied, averting her gaze. "Nobody is going to risk getting on the coach's bad side. He was clear that no one could intervene in your punishment. We're pushing it as it is."

Camila sighed. "I really messed up."

"Yeah. I don't get what happened."

"Antonia just gets on my nerves."

Liz threw her a sympathetic look that only made her feel worse.

"The fact that I'll have to watch her start the game tomorrow while I stay on the bench, then go share a room with her afterward, is adding insult to injury. I can only imagine how smug she'll be. It's going to take all my willpower to not react."

"Fighting with her won't do anything to help you get on the team."

"I know," Camila said, and she sighed again.

"What's up with you two, anyway? I've never seen you act like this before."

"She just has a way of getting under my skin."

Liz raised her eyebrows, though she didn't press. Camila opened her mouth but closed it without saying another word. She couldn't explain why Antonia affected her so much. Maybe it was because she never backed down and never seemed afraid to call her out. And there was also their night together. It made Camila feel stupid and vulnerable, and she hated feeling that way. Keeping Antonia at arm's length was safer than risking falling for her infuriating charm again.

She didn't tell Liz what had happened between her and Antonia. If she shared that information, everyone would assume their fight was nothing more than hurt feelings after a one-night stand. Besides, it was never happening again. There was no point in bringing it up when what she wanted was to forget about that lapse in judgment.

Camila glanced at her watch and let out a groan. It was only 6:00 p.m. It would be at least four or five more hours before she dared step into her own room.

95

Antonia dropped her bag on top of the bed and left the hotel room as soon as possible. She didn't want to run into Sánchez, so she decided that the best course of action was to stay away. No matter how hot Sánchez was, it wasn't worth the hassle. Antonia was in Houston for work. To turn her dreams into reality. She could do without all the drama, and if avoiding her hotel room for the weekend was the price she had to pay, she would do it.

At least she had López to keep her company. It may have started as a joke, but López was becoming one of her best friends. She was thankful when López didn't question her when she said she needed to stay out of her room.

"Are you gonna tell me why we're hiding in the hotel lobby instead of resting in our rooms?" López said without looking away from her phone.

"You know why," Antonia stated plainly.

"I know you don't want to see Sánchez, but I don't know why you two have been avoiding each other like the plague."

Antonia shot her an indignant look that was promptly ignored. "Weren't you standing right there when we had a fight in the middle of practice? I think I remember you trying to step between us."

"Yes, I remember that." López looked up. "Again, I know you had a fight, but I still don't know what caused it or why you refuse to get over it."

"I should get over it? She's the one attacking me for no reason all the time. Because, I don't know, she is so conceited she can't deal with the fact that I'm a better player than her? I'm over it. I refuse to make it easy for her." As she spoke, her voice became louder.

"Wow. Okay, my bad." López put her hands up in mock surrender, but her smirk made it obvious she wasn't sorry at all. "I feel like that's not the complete story, though . . . You tapped that, didn't you?"

Antonia hoped her face didn't give her away because she had no intention of admitting to anyone what had happened between them. For one, she didn't see any need. For two, if Sánchez somehow found out she was talking about the topic, she would have a fit and take it out on her.

"She wishes." Antonia scoffed. "Maybe it's that repressed energy that makes her so stuck-up all the time."

"If you don't want to tell me, that's fine. But I know sexual tension when I see it, and she looks at you like a scorned ex. Did you run away without saying goodbye?"

"I think she looks at everyone like that. And I would never do that. You always get breakfast after sex with me; I'm considerate like that."

"Does that mean I have to sleep with you to get some food around here? It better be good."

"I'm an excellent cook. You get privileges, so I will buy you dinner just for being a good sport about all this. Sorry, you'll have to miss out on the sex part."

"That's fine. Better to not ruin our friendship. I know if you get a piece of this"—López pointed at her ass—"you could never leave."

Antonia chuckled. "Let's go. I owe you dinner."

"Camila, please. It's eleven, and I'm sleepy. You're going to have to face Antonia eventually."

"Eventually doesn't have to mean tonight." Camila glanced at her watch for the hundredth time in half an hour. "Okay, I guess it's late enough she could be sleeping. Here goes nothing." If even Liz was over her, Camila had no other option but to go to her room.

Liz climbed into bed and turned away from her. "Good. Please turn off the lights on the way out."

It took Camila less than two minutes to reach her room, but she stood outside of it for what felt like an eternity. She fidgeted with the string of her sweatpants and put her ear close to the door, worried she would run into Antonia despite all her efforts.

To her relief, darkness and silence greeted her when she opened the door. The bag lying on top of one of the beds was the only evidence that Antonia had been there. Camila pushed down the sudden rush of disappointment she felt at not running into Antonia. This was what she wanted.

She placed her bag on the other bed, but instead of changing into her pajamas and getting under the covers, she headed to the shower. Showering at night always relaxed her.

While the hot water dripped down her neck and back, she tried to clear her mind. To let the water be a symbol of washing away the stress she'd felt all day. She stayed under the spray of water until her hands wrinkled and her eyelids felt heavy. It was the most relaxed she'd felt in a while—but the sound of a creaking door chased the sleepiness away.

She listened as nimble steps moved around the room, opening and closing drawers. It had to be Antonia on the other side of the bathroom door, which created a dilemma. Camila could pretend to shower for as long as necessary, hoping Antonia went to bed and fell asleep soon. Or she could go out and face the inevitable.

She cursed under her breath and wrapped the tiny hotel towel around herself. It wasn't the best outfit to have on for a potential run-in with Antonia, but her only other option was to stay trapped in the bathroom forever. With one last deep breath, she turned the knob.

Antonia was facing away from her, wearing the shortest shorts Camila had ever seen, and she had her back exposed. Camila lost herself in the way Antonia's delts and upper-back muscles flexed when she leaned down to pick up a shirt from her luggage. She'd seen Antonia naked a couple of days before, had seen a lot more than what was exposed in that moment. Still, she couldn't help but stare as if it were the first time, unable to tear her eyes away until Antonia finished putting on her shirt.

Thankfully, Camila's bed was the one closer to the bathroom. In two steps she was next to it, opening her suitcase to search for some clothes to wear. The towel didn't make it easy. She kept having to readjust it with one hand as it threatened to slip off at any second with every movement she made.

At one point she felt Antonia's eyes on her, but when she raised her head to look in her direction, Antonia averted her gaze. Camila didn't. She couldn't look away even if she wanted. The small, tight pajamas Antonia was wearing brought back images she'd been trying to forget.

If her gaze bothered her, Antonia didn't show it. She turned away from Camila, almost as if she didn't exist. Camila realized that if she wanted to fix things between them, she had to do it right then. She knew without a doubt that if they went to sleep without talking, Antonia wouldn't be there by the time Camila woke up. It was obvious they had both been avoiding each other equally.

She tightened the towel around her body once more and walked closer to Antonia's side of the room. "Can we talk?"

When Antonia didn't answer or even acknowledge her, Camila pushed her annoyance down. The goal was to fix things, not to make them worse. She tried again.

"Look, I understand if you don't want to talk to me, but I want to come to a truce. This situation is not beneficial for either of us," she said, then paused to see if Antonia reacted.

Still nothing.

"We're adults. I think we can put everything behind us and both admit we made mistakes."

Antonia turned around, finally looking at Camila. "We both made mistakes?"

"Yes. But as I was saying, I think we can look past them," Camila said, trying to keep the anger that was rising inside her again out of her voice.

Antonia took a step in her direction with her hands on her hips. "I'm happy to leave things behind us if you admit that it was your fault. Not once have I heard you apologize."

"My fault? I think we're equally at fault here."

Antonia took another step toward Camila. "You attacked me during an entire practice. Shoved me, faulted me, and did everything in your power to get in my way for absolutely no reason. I only reacted, and I won't apologize for that."

"Attacked you for no reason?" Camila said, voice raised. "I had every reason in the world. You've done nothing but play with me, judge me, and steal my place on the team."

"All those are made-up reasons you invented out of, I don't know, jealousy?"

"Oh, please!" Camila scoffed. "Don't flatter yourself. I couldn't care less about what you do and with who."

Antonia smirked, and Camila realized she'd slipped up.

"Jealousy about me being on the starter team," Antonia said. "I thought we agreed it was a fun night and nothing else."

"Yeah, that's what I was talking about. The team. And it's ridiculous you think I'm jealous of that. I know I'm as good as anyone on the team."

"You know, that's your problem. Being part of a team is not about proving how good you are. It's about working together for the one common goal we all have: to win." Antonia's voice became softer as she spoke. "Maybe if you spent more time trying to help the team instead of trying to prove yourself, Coach Medina would see how you fit and what you can add."

Camila looked down, mulling over Antonia's words. They made sense; she knew they did. But she refused to back down. "That's what I'm doing. Showing that I'm good helps the team."

"Whatever," Antonia answered, and started to turn away again.

"Wait!" Camila stepped closer. "What I wanted to say was . . . I'm sorry. As you said, we both want the same thing, for the team to win and succeed. I should have handled things better."

Antonia looked at her with an unreadable expression on her face. "Go on," she said in a flat tone.

Camila gritted her teeth and swallowed the reply building up. Of course Antonia wouldn't make it easy for her.

"I think it would be to everyone's benefit if we forgot about our disagreements and started again with a clean slate," Camila said instead. "I hope we can at least maintain a civil and professional relationship if you're willing."

That was it. She had pushed her pride aside to fix things. Now it was Antonia's turn.

"I only want to play football. That's all I care about," Antonia replied. "So sure, I'm happy to put everything that happened in the past couple of days behind us."

A weight lifted from Camila's shoulders, but she expected an apology in return, and it didn't look like Antonia was about to offer her one.

"Great . . . Isn't there more you'd like to tell me?" she said.

"Hmm . . . I don't think so."

Camila answered Antonia's words with a strained smile. She extended her hand outward. "Peace?"

Antonia glanced down at her hand and back up at her face. A second later, she shook it. "To a new beginning," she said, pulling Camila toward her. "And I'm sorry too," she whispered.

Camila nodded but didn't let go of Antonia's hand. The sudden touch of their skin and the warmth of Antonia's body took her back to memories of pleasure and ecstasy. It was just a hand. It shouldn't create that reaction. But the moment their bodies touched, electricity shot from her fingertips to every cell in her body. She hated the effect Antonia had on her. She wanted it to be anyone else but her, but of course in a team full of beautiful queer women, she was attracted to the one who infuriated her without even trying.

As soon as Antonia moved her hand away, Camila missed the contact, but it was also a relief. She wasn't sure what would happen if they didn't step away from each other. Since her muscles had lost the ability to move, it was down to Antonia to put distance between them.

Camila watched as the other girl licked her lips while looking at her, and her own heart rate increased in response. She both craved and dreaded a kiss. But Antonia turned away instead, crushing the hopes she didn't realize she harbored.

When Antonia walked to her bed, Camila followed behind her. She was acting on instinct. Her mind screamed at her to go to her own bed, but her body was pulled toward Antonia. She gripped her arm and turned her around. As soon as their eyes met, Camila grabbed Antonia's face with both of her hands and crushed their lips together.

Antonia knew it was a bad idea. The worst idea in the world. She knew it, but she did nothing to stop it. The moment Sánchez's lips found hers, their fates were sealed. There was no way she could drag herself away when the taste was so good, when her body was set on fire by one touch.

She didn't know what made Sánchez so enticing, so intoxicating. Her touch was like gas to a flame. Each one of Antonia's senses heightened around her, be it under rough caresses or icy stares. It had taken all her strength to step away a minute before, thinking Sánchez wouldn't want her. But now she realized that as much as Sánchez tried to hate her, she craved as much as Antonia did.

She brought Sánchez toward her with a firm yank on her waist. Their bodies collided, merging into one, with only the thin cotton of Antonia's shirt and the small towel barely hanging over Sánchez's body as a barrier between them.

When they broke apart, Sánchez's ragged breath hit Antonia's face like a warm sea breeze, and hungry eyes stared back at her. For a second, she saw a hint of hesitation in those hazel eyes. Sánchez moved her hands off Antonia's face. She leaned away as if afraid of Antonia's reaction. As if it wasn't obvious how much Antonia wanted her, how it was impossible for her to resist. Even when they fought, even when she found Sánchez infuriating, she still wanted her.

Antonia realized that they both were afraid of the same thing—of giving too much of themselves to someone when they didn't know how much they would get in return.

"I want you," she mumbled. Maybe it wasn't much, but those three simple words had to be enough at that moment. "Do you want me?"

"I do," Sánchez answered, her hands cradling Antonia's face again.

Antonia let out a sigh. A weight she hadn't realized she'd been carrying left her chest. They walked backward, connected in a slow, measured kiss until Sánchez's legs hit the bed frame and stopped them. Antonia simply pushed Sánchez to make her fall on top of the mattress. She followed, climbing on top, her knees and hands trapping the girl under her. A small mole on Sánchez's left boob, suddenly uncovered after the towel fell off her body, captured Antonia's attention. It called her like a bullseye. She licked her lips in anticipation while she leaned down with only one objective in mind. She sucked on the mole and kissed it, before following the path to the perky brown nipple below it.

Sánchez held Antonia's head in place as she circled the sensitive area with the tip of her tongue. Hands grasped her harder, pushing her closer as she alternated the measured licks with deep, strong sucking and soft teeth raking up and down the erect little nub in her mouth.

She moved down Sánchez's body, repeating the same pattern and getting the same reaction. Moans, sighs, and a firm hand that was tangled in her curls pushed Antonia further south. She couldn't wait to taste her, to have her come undone again, to have her one more time.

She kissed Sánchez's firm abdomen and then moved to the tattoo on the left side of her rib cage. A single sentence in beautiful cursive calligraphy hugged her curves. Antonia tried to focus on kissing, on enjoying the body under her grasp, but the tattoo kept calling to her. Maybe because it was another way to delve into Sánchez's guarded mind without having to ask anything.

She moved her kisses up and to the side, getting closer and closer to the letters. Once she reached them, she traced them with her tongue and kissed the thorns of the rose painted on Sánchez's side. How fitting that she'd chosen something so prickly to adorn her body.

Antonia left her thoughts behind when Sánchez's insistent hand pushed her head down again. She smirked but stopped herself from making a joke, afraid it would ruin the mood. Although Sánchez's nudge wasn't rough or demanding, Antonia understood what it meant. She would give her what she wanted soon, but not yet.

She grabbed Sánchez's thighs and held her in place as her mouth followed the path of her skin. She kissed her legs, her stomach, the inside of her thighs, getting closer and closer to where Antonia knew Sánchez craved to be touched. Her shallow exhales caressed Sánchez's Mound of Venus, leaving a trail of goose bumps behind. She breathed closer and closer, her lips hovering right above the skin without touching it, until she couldn't take it any longer. Intoxicated by the smell of sex and need, she buried her face in Sánchez, inhaled her essence, and let her tongue wander around the wet folds.

Antonia stopped the teasing and let herself enjoy the sweet taste on her tongue as Sánchez's moans and sighs became music to her ears. There was nothing she enjoyed more than knowing she was the reason someone was coming unraveled. Every moan, every whimper filled her with satisfaction. She didn't want it to end, wanted to drag it out as much as she could. She ran her tongue over the nub of nerves, but as soon as Sánchez's ragged breathing increased, as soon as her moans became more frequent, as soon as she asked for more, Antonia moved away to kiss around the area. Sánchez's pointed groan only made her smile.

She did the same thing once, twice, three times. Every time she gave more attention to Sánchez's center, but she still moved away. She was about to do it again when Sánchez said, "I swear to God, Carvalho, if you dare stop again . . ."

Antonia grinned but listened and didn't move away again until Sánchez's hands clutched her back and her moans were so loud, they could probably be heard from the hotel lobby. Afterward, she climbed up again to meet Sánchez's lips.

To her surprise, Sánchez deepened the kiss and switched their positions. Antonia returned her advances with enthusiasm. She would take as much as she could get while she could get it, since she didn't know what the next day might bring for them. If Sánchez would go back to ignoring her.

Chapter Nine

ANTONIA HATED THE TWINGE of disappointment she felt at waking up alone. She didn't expect them to cuddle and whisper sweet nothings to each other, but she'd hoped they could at least move on from the avoiding and the tension. She stretched her aching muscles, smiled at the memory of the night before and wondered, not for the first time, why Sánchez fascinated her so much.

She'd had her share of relationships in her life, but she'd never felt the pull she did with Sánchez. It had always been easy to step away, to put the women in her life second when she needed to. With Sánchez, it was a constant struggle to keep her distance, and she'd already failed twice.

She shook her head, trying to push the thoughts away. Her time would be better spent getting ready for their upcoming match, instead of dwelling on a woman who couldn't run away from her fast enough as soon as they were done having sex.

Antonia was getting dressed after a quick shower when the room's door opened and Sánchez walked in with a Starbucks bag in her hand. They both froze in place, their eyes meeting across the room.

"You trying to steal my move, Carvalho?" Sánchez said, looking her up and down.

Antonia laughed, surprised at the lightheartedness of Sánchez's tone. "I'm not letting this towel drop. We don't have time for that."

"That's a shame, but agreed. I don't want another lecture from Coach Medina, even if he was the one who told us to get along." She raised the paper bag. "I ran to get some coffee and brought you breakfast."

There was still some tension in the air—as if each was expecting the other to blow up at any second and destroy the tentative truce they'd established. Their hesitance around each other was a stark contrast to their actions from the night before. It was a start, though. Almost a peace offering. Antonia would take it.

"You're a lifesaver. I'm starving." She grabbed the bag with one hand while the other stayed in place on top of the towel to prevent a slip-up, causing a smirk to spread over Sánchez's lips. Antonia thought she looked even more beautiful when she relaxed.

The bag ended up abandoned on top of the bedside table while she stared at her clothes arranged on top of the bed. Normally, she would sit on the bed naked to dry herself before getting dressed, but with Sánchez standing right next to her, she wasn't sure what to do. Nakedness didn't embarrass her, but Sánchez's stare confused her. She looked back and forth between the clothes and the other woman. When Sánchez showed no intention of leaving or turning around, Antonia dropped the towel and reached for her panties on the bed.

Sánchez let out a little yelp, covered her eyes with her hand, and turned around in one swift motion. "Sorry. You probably want some privacy."

"I assumed you wanted a show. I promise to make it a better one next time." Antonia snickered. Maybe she enjoyed messing with her a little too much.

She was in the middle of putting on her shirt when Sánchez turned around again. She glanced down, avoiding her eyes, but it didn't appear to be out of embarrassment over Antonia's state of undress.

"Next time, huh?" Sánchez said.

Antonia noticed that she was playing with the bottom of her shirt. The change in attitude confused her, and as much as she tried to guess what was going through Sánchez's mind, she couldn't imagine what it was.

"I'm not saying it will happen again, but I'm not opposed to it," Antonia said. "If one day you want to and it happens, it happens. I'm a go-with-the-flow kind of person."

Sánchez let out a soft chuckle. "Yeah, I've noticed that." She stopped messing with her shirt, and her gaze found Antonia's eyes. "This may be the worst idea I've ever had, but it seems like we get along a lot better when we're having sex, so I was thinking . . ."

Antonia nodded when Sánchez trailed off but said nothing.

"Forget about it, it's ridiculous. I'll see you downstairs." Sánchez snatched up her bag and walked toward the door.

Antonia grabbed her arm before she could bolt out of the room. "You want to keep having sex with me, is that it? 'Cause yeah, that would be cool," she said with a shrug.

Sánchez's eyes widened, and she ran a hand through her hair. "I don't know if I should be glad or mortified at how direct you are."

"If I'm right, you should be glad 'cause we can avoid the awkwardness of dancing around each other and have fun instead."

"Okay. Yeah, I would like for what happened last night to happen again."

"Perfect. We can sort out the details later. We're running late, but friends with benefits it is," Antonia said, offering her hand for a handshake.

Sánchez took it. "We're not friends, but yes to the benefits part."

Antonia used their joint hands to pull Sánchez toward her for a short but passionate kiss. "Sorry, the handshake felt weird." She smiled.

Sánchez shook her head but leaned forward for another brief kiss. "See you downstairs."

Camila sat at the back of the bus and watched as Antonia greeted López with a bump on the shoulder and her characteristic sonorous laugh. It all seemed so normal. As if fifteen minutes before, they hadn't been in their room, agreeing to a casual sex relationship. She scoffed under her breath. If only their teammates knew about it. They would never believe it. But the more Camila thought about it, the more it made sense.

"Both of you are still alive. That's progress," Liz said from her spot next to Camila.

"Yeah, we cleared things up last night. I think we'll be able to keep the peace."

"From the rumors going around, you did way more than keep the peace." Liz waggled her eyebrows and smirked. "When I heard about it, I thought they'd mixed up the sounds of you two killing each other, but now I see it was the opposite."

Camila rolled her eyes. "She is way less annoying when I make sure her mouth is busy. That's all." She put on her headphones.

Without meaning to, her gaze landed on Antonia. She fought to look away, but her eyes were stuck watching the way Antonia casually wrapped her arm over López's shoulders. And for a second, she wished she was sitting next to her instead.

"That's all, huh? You're going to burn a hole through her head with that staring," Liz said.

"I'm just annoyed at how loud she is. Some of us would like a chance to focus."

Camila hit Play on her phone, turning away to stare through the window while the sounds of "Haven't Had Enough" by Marianas Trench filled her headphones. For a second, the music gave her the refuge she needed, until the words hit too close to home and she tapped her headphones to skip ahead. She already knew her attraction to Antonia was ill-advised. There was no need for a song to remind her.

She closed her eyes and visualized the upcoming match. She wasn't a starter, but since it was a friendly game, there was a big possibility of being subbed in for the second half. If so, she wanted to use the chance to show Coach Medina why she deserved to be on the starting lineup. In her mind, she dominated the midfield, filtering precise long passes between the defenders to set up goals for the team and kicking the free throws and corner kicks with flawless precision, just like her dad did when he was a player.

A tap on her shoulder shook her out of the daydream.

"Hey there."

Camila turned around with lightning speed, only to wish her eyes could shoot laser beams out of them—although she had a feeling even that wouldn't faze Antonia. The unwavering grin on Antonia's face, despite Camila's angry stare, was proof of it.

Camila clenched her jaw. "Why are you sitting next to me?"

"Because I want to."

"Well, move. I don't want to give people ideas."

Antonia tilted her head to the side. "I don't think anyone will realize we're sleeping together just because I sat next to you on the bus."

Camila elbowed Antonia harder than she intended, but the small groan she was met with caused her enormous satisfaction. "They will if you keep announcing it at the top of your lungs."

"Sorry, I didn't realize this was a secret affair. If you ask me, your exaggerated annoyance with me only makes it more obvious."

"It's not exaggerated. If anything, I'm doing an amazing job of controlling my disdain for you." She sneered, but it didn't have any bite to it.

"Well, if it makes you feel better, I'm only sitting next to you because your friend asked to switch places. I guess I can see why, since you're being such a ray of sunshine."

Camila glanced ahead and noticed Liz chatting with López a few rows up. She frowned at the faint blush on her friend's cheeks and wondered why Liz had ditched her. Granted, she hadn't planned on talking to her at all; she wanted to lose herself in her music and ignore everything around her, but that didn't mean Liz had to move away, much less switch places with the person she wanted around the least. Even with their recent arrangement, Antonia's closeness still put her on edge.

"Why would she do that?" Camila muttered to herself.

"Oh, they're sleeping together . . . or want to."

Camila shot daggers at her. "I thought sitting next to each other meant nothing."

"Well, I don't think every single person on this bus is sleeping with whoever is sitting next to them right now. Like, I sure as hell hope Coach Megan has better taste than Coach Medina. But Young and López are." Antonia leaned in as if she wanted to share a secret, and Camila moved closer too. "And so are we," she whispered.

Camila moved away with a frown, and Antonia laughed.

"I'll leave you alone so you can focus," she added.

While Camila stared at her, Antonia reached into her bag for a tablet, not bothering to look at her again. Which was what Camila preferred. She could handle sitting next to her if she left her alone.

Camila turned away and hit Play on her phone again, but as much as she wanted to, she couldn't go back to visualizing the upcoming match. The entire ride to the stadium, she was aware of Antonia's body next to hers—the heat emanating from her, as well as her slow, measured breathing.

Knowing ahead of time she was starting the game on the bench didn't make things any less disappointing for Camila. She sat in a corner in her sweats, looking at her teammates with a mix of sadness and bitterness as they ran to the field. Her eyes fixed on Antonia the most because she was her biggest competition. Not for any other reason. Of course not. If she stared at her tan legs, it was only because she didn't want to miss any of her movements—not because she thought they were beautiful or because flashes were going through her mind of those same legs wrapped around her waist.

Her interest, at least in that moment, was purely professional. Coach Medina opted for a 4-3-3 formation with Antonia as a left winger. It made sense to take advantage of her speed and the fact that she was left-handed. Camila preferred to play as a pure forward, waiting for passes in the goal area.

Camila couldn't help but think they would make a great attacking duo as she watched Antonia run down the band and leave one, two, three opposing players behind. She sent a pass directly to the middle of the penalty area, only for López to miss the goal shot.

On the next attack, Antonia moved from the left to the right side of the field, surprising the defender by running toward the center and dribbling to set up a direct shot on the goal instead of a pass. The shot cruised above everyone's heads and passed the goalkeeper's extended hands, to end up in the left corner for their first goal.

"Yes!" Coach Medina exclaimed. "That girl is worth her weight in gold," he added, hitting Coach Megan on the back.

While Camila was in the middle of celebrating, the coach's words sunk in, instantly ending her excitement. She doubted he would ever say something like that about her. He didn't even think she was good enough to start the game. She sat in the corner again, this time barely paying attention to the match.

Her disappointment only grew when she remained on the bench, despite the team having five substitutions available. The coach only made two at halftime, one to try the second goalkeeper and another in the midfield, and she wasn't one of them. If she wasn't good enough for a practice game, what were the odds of her getting to play consistently once the season started?

"Sánchez, start warming up."

"Wha . . . Yes, Coach," she replied, caught off guard by the abrupt order.

There were only ten minutes left in the match, but she would take them.

She jumped on the field with a fast sprint from the sidelines to the center. It was a way to help her muscles activate and show everyone how ready she was to play. For the first few minutes, she saw little action—a touch here and there, and running to cover spaces in defense when the other team recovered the ball. Both teams fought for possession in the middle of the field until a steal from López caught the other team by surprise.

Camila ran toward the opposite goal as soon as she saw López looking up to see what options she had for a pass. As soon as she received the ball, two defenders closed in on her, but she saw Antonia out of the corner of her eye. With one precise pass between the defenders' legs, Camila sent the ball to her feet. Antonia didn't hesitate to take a powerful long-distance shot that the goalkeeper couldn't stop.

Antonia ran in her direction, and Camila reacted on instinct when the other girl jumped into her arms and wrapped her legs around her waist in a full-body hug. She was so happy about the goal and her great assist that, for a second, she forgot she wanted to keep her distance from Antonia in public. Soon the effervescence of the goal faded away, and the heat of Antonia's body became more obvious, at least to her. Antonia still seemed lost in the euphoria of scoring. Thankfully, their teammates joined them soon enough, and they separated to high-five and celebrate with the rest of the team.

The match finished shortly after, but the high from a job well done never left Camila's body. As she walked toward the locker room, she was still buzzing with energy.

"Good job, Sánchez. That pass was a beauty," the coach said to her as she passed him. The words made her chest swell with pride and a smile appear on her lips.

Antonia's breath tickled her ear with a whisper. "Yes, good job, Sánchez." She moved away just as fast as she'd approached, leaving a trail of goose bumps on Camila's skin.

Half an hour later, right as Camila was about to board the team's bus, the coach approached her.

"Sánchez, I need to talk with you for a second."

Camila did her best to stop the grin threatening to take over her face. As she'd hoped, her performance hadn't gone unnoticed. "Sure thing, Coach."

"You did good today," he said. "Carvalho and you seem to get along now, which is great. Players complementing each other can do magic for a team."

She frowned at the mention of Antonia. "Yeah, I guess we worked well together."

"It gave me an idea. As part of Carvalho's contract, the team has to provide her with a place to stay. She has been at a downtown hotel for the past couple of weeks, but they're having trouble finding a more permanent place, so they've decided that some players will have to share apartments while they sort everything out."

"Okay . . ." Camila answered, not sure what her coach was getting at. She also had a place provided by the team.

"If you ask me, they're probably just being cheap. It's not like women's soccer gets the money it needs. But anyway, they asked me to help them sort out who should stay with who, and I think you two should share. Getting along on and off the field can strengthen a team. After seeing what you two can do playing together, it's in our best interest that you two get along."

Camila wanted to scream. Suddenly, she was being upgraded from bench player to sidekick, but only because of a chance good pass to Antonia. Living with Antonia was a recipe for disaster and the last thing she wanted, but there was no way to explain to him why it wasn't a good idea.

"Hmm . . . I think Antonia gets along better with López," she said. "They seem to have hit it off from the start."

The expression in Coach Medina's eyes changed, his disappointment becoming clear. The last thing Camila wanted was to ruin her chance at making a good impression.

"But if you think it's better if we live together, I'm happy to share an apartment with her," she added.

"Great. You're a team player. That's what I like."

The coach walked away and boarded the bus. Camila let out a groan before following him.

Chapter Ten

THE NEWS ABOUT THE change in her living arrangements came as a surprise, but Antonia couldn't be happier about leaving behind the constant mold smell of her hotel room. She had no clue why Coach Medina had decided that she and Camila should live together; she wondered if it was a way to extend their punishment for the altercation they had in practice, or a misguided attempt to force them to get along.

The moving happened fast, what with all her belongings fitting in two suitcases. López insisted on helping her, which she appreciated. If nothing else, it kept her from having to immediately be alone with Sánchez, who had been in an awful mood since they got the news of their updated living situation.

"This is the easiest move I've ever been to," López exclaimed once they finished arranging Antonia's clothes in the closet.

"I told you it would be."

"To be honest, I only came for the pizza afterward."

Antonia opened the delivery app on her phone. "One Hawaiian pizza coming right up!"

"Don't you dare! That's an abomination."

"The only thing that's an abomination is how limited the pizza choices are here. If you ever go to Brazil, I'll take you to eat pizza. Dessert pizza is the best! My favorite has pineapple, peach, fig, strawberries, and condensed milk. You're missing out, I tell you." Antonia wanted to burst out laughing at López's horrified face. She loved Hawaiian pizza, and she wouldn't let anyone stop her from ordering one. "I'll order something else for you. Boring pepperoni sound good?"

"Anything but that atrocity you just mentioned. Now you're going to say you love anchovies too."

"I prefer our canned tuna pizza, but the one time I tried anchovies, I loved them."

López raised her hands in an I-give-up gesture. "I don't know what to say. Next time, I'm ordering the pizza, that's all."

Antonia cracked up. "Don't worry. I'll get something appropriate for your refined palate."

The sound of gunshots and explosions mixed with Sánchez's voice as Antonia and López walked the couple of steps separating her bedroom from the living room. She wanted to ask López if they could stay in her room, but before she could, the other girl settled on the sofa right next to Young. There was no other option but to follow suit. Antonia sat on the floor between López's legs and looked at the TV right in time to see a poor guy being blown apart. Young and López echoed her groan, while Sánchez chuckled.

"Oh, come on, guys. *Zombieland* is a classic," Sánchez exclaimed.

"I'm more of a Disney fan myself," Antonia mumbled.

Everyone turned to stare at her.

"What?"

"You're a Disney fan?"

She shrugged. "Yeah. My mom would buy bootlegs for me and my brother to watch while she worked late. *Toy Story* is my favorite, but I've watched all their animated movies at least ten times each."

She didn't understand why everyone was looking at her with confused expressions. What was so strange about her liking Disney movies?

"Once I'm more settled and have enough money to pay for it, I'm going to take my brother to Disney World. It's been our dream since we were kids," she added.

López broke the silence. "I never pegged you as a Disney fan, but that's cute."

Another gunshot coming from the TV pulled attention away from her. She looked at the screen too, for lack of anything better to do, but she felt a pair of eyes burning a hole in the back of her head. Curiosity won over, and she turned around, only to be met by Sánchez's stare. There was a softness to them, a tenderness that was new, but Sánchez looked away before Antonia could decipher what it meant.

A notification on her phone alerted Antonia to the arrival of their pizza. She took on the duty of handing out plates and serving drinks to everyone. The first bite of her Hawaiian pizza tasted like glory, but it was missing something. She rummaged in the kitchen drawers until she found a small packet of ketchup.

As she drizzled the ketchup on another piece of pizza, all eyes focused on her, but she ignored them in favor of taking another bite.

"What?" she said with her mouth half-full.

"What are you doing?" López cried. "Pineapple on pizza wasn't enough of a sacrilege that you had to go and add ketchup?"

She finished chewing. "I know. I prefer mustard, but ketchup is pretty good too."

López's eyes widened even more. "You're close to ruining the one thing that motivated me to help you. It's really hard to ruin pizza, but you're almost there."

"I got you a different pizza, and I'm not forcing you to add ketchup to it!" Antonia took another slice and drizzled the last of the packet on it. "Besides, we all know you came because you wanted an excuse to hang out with Young."

López's face flushed slightly. "I don't need an excuse to hang out with Liz. If I want to see her, I can ask her. We aren't pretending to hate each other like you and Camila."

Young elbowed López, but the words were already out. Antonia didn't care what her teammates said or thought about them, but she could see the tension in Sánchez's neck and the way she avoided her eyes. Living together was going to be hard enough without López butting in with unnecessary comments.

Antonia mustered the sweetest, fakest smile she could. "You need to catch up, López. Sánchez and I are the best of friends now."

López crossed her arms. "Is that so?"

"Yeah. We get along great, and my favorite thing about her is that she minds her own damn business instead of butting into someone else's."

López let out a laugh. "This is how you thank me for helping you."

"You barely did anything," Antonia answered.

The rest of the afternoon went smoothly. They watched more movies, played Uno, and ate pizza until their bellies hurt. For the first time since she'd arrived, Antonia felt like maybe she could build a home in Houston after all.

Even Sánchez had dropped the sour mood and laughed along with them when López tried to cheat to win at Uno. Antonia thought things were good between them until Sánchez locked herself in her room the minute they were alone.

Instead of knocking on her door like she wanted to, Antonia busied herself with cleaning up the remnants of the afternoon that were scattered around the apartment and taking a shower to relax her muscles. As she walked to her room from the bathroom, her feet took her to Sánchez's door before she realized it. For a long minute, she held her clenched fist in the air, inches away from the solid wood separating them.

Through the door, she heard the faint sound of Sánchez's even breathing. After a few more minutes, she walked away.

When the smell of pancakes and bacon failed to elicit a reaction, Antonia knocked on Sánchez's door, only to find the bed empty when she dared to push the door open. Sánchez had already left.

The disappointment of waking up to an empty apartment settled in her stomach for only a second before she shrugged it off. If Sánchez wanted to act like a guest in her own home just to avoid her, there was nothing she could do about it. She hadn't forced Sánchez to agree to live with her. If she had a problem with it, she could take it to the coach or to team management.

Those thoughts didn't stop her from saving the leftovers in a Tupperware and leaving a note on top of it. *In case you get hungry . . . I promise I didn't poison it.*

It was one of those rare days off from training, and Antonia was itching to go out after spending the previous day trapped in the apartment. She grabbed her running shoes and took an Uber to Memorial Park. It was early enough that the heat was still manageable and with the right music selection flowing from her earbuds, she could almost imagine she was running along the Florianópolis beaches instead of being in the middle of the city.

As if he'd been reading her mind, her phone rang in that exact moment with a call from her brother. She smiled on reflex. As soon as she hit Answer and the sound of falling pots filled her ears, her mind conjured up an image of him hiding in the resort restaurant pantry to have a few minutes to talk to her.

"I hope lunch is safe," she said.

"Eh, the tourists will survive with one less pot of shrimp," he answered, and Antonia could almost see the bright grin and glinting eyes he must have had in that moment.

"I'm sure you'll charm them if they complain."

"You know it. Just as I'm sure you've already charmed everyone there."

Sánchez's face flashed through Antonia's head. "It's okay. The coach seems to like me, and I've earned a spot on the team. That's all that matters."

"As your older brother, I shouldn't encourage partying or anything like that, but don't get too caught up in work. Remember to have fun."

"I always have fun when I'm playing," Antonia retorted.

"You know that's not what I mean."

"I've made a couple of friends, I swear. They don't hold a candle to you, though."

"Of course they don't, but they'll do until I'm able to get there."

Antonia smiled to herself. She couldn't wait to have him here. To drive him around and hand him the keys and the lease to his own restaurant. A place where his talents could shine.

"Or maybe I could take you to France with me instead," he added.

"France?"

"There's this scholarship my boss is encouraging me to apply to. It covers a year of culinary school in France, and they would help me get a part-time job to cover living expenses."

"That's amazing!"

"I mean, I doubt I'll get it. But no harm in trying, right?"

"You should go for it." She grinned, even though he couldn't see it. "You deserve to live your dreams too."

Camila had to leave. It didn't matter that it was six in the morning when she opened her eyes. As soon as sleep faded away and she remembered that Antonia was in the bedroom next to hers, the urge to escape became unbearable.

She put on the first pair of shorts she found and her favorite tank top. Walking out of the apartment, she wasn't sure where she was going. She just needed to put distance between them. Though she wasn't sure what would happen if she didn't, she feared it would end up with her in Antonia's arms again, between her legs, under her weight. As good as it felt in the moment, it had happened too many times already for her to pretend it meant nothing—though she would still try. She would never admit it out loud to anyone else, but she hated how Antonia could break down her defenses without even trying, every single time.

The gym in the apartment building became her refuge. Camila ran on the treadmill, mixing short sprints with a few seconds of rest to simulate the reality of a soccer game. She lifted weights, did squats, and used every single machine available to her until her muscles burned with effort.

She sat on a free-weight bench, arms resting on her knees. It was nine o'clock, and she didn't think her body could take any more punishment. She'd have to face Antonia sooner or later. She hoped by the time she made it back, the other girl would be gone, but she knew it was more likely she'd find her at ease, enjoying her new home. Unlike her, Antonia didn't seem to care about being around her. Not that she wanted Antonia to want her around, but it would be nice to not be the only one whose world had turned upside down when they met.

Her phone ended up being her last refuge in her quest to delay the inevitable. A text from her dad was waiting for her.

How's my princess? Making Dad proud on her new team?

She shot a quick reply to him, telling him about how things weren't exactly going to plan, what with her sitting on the bench most of the time.

Camila then opened a message from her mom, who was apparently trying to set her up with some model from her agency.

We just need a couple of pictures to put him on the map. Let me know next time you're in LA so we can arrange it.

She ignored it. As usual, her mom only reached out when she needed something.

She considered texting Liz to ask if she could hide at her apartment, but avoiding Antonia wasn't a sustainable strategy. She'd also already bothered Liz enough, between crashing her hotel room in San Diego and forcing her to be there the day before so she didn't have to be alone with Antonia. She took a deep breath and went to the elevator.

The apartment was quiet when she walked in, with no trace of Antonia except for the subtle smell of food lingering in the air. A Tupperware with a note on it sat in the fridge. She opened it, and her mouth watered at the sight. The first bite of pancake almost melted in her mouth, the sweetness of the maple syrup coating her tongue.

She hated how, despite everything, Antonia was still nice to her. How she still tried. It made it harder to keep her at arm's length. Harder to remember that she meant nothing to Antonia beyond a fun time, and she shouldn't read much into her random acts of kindness. It was easier to push her away than to believe they could become friends. Having her around all the time would be torture, but maybe if she reminded herself that Antonia didn't want her, she could stay away.

When Antonia returned from her run, Sánchez was standing in the kitchen wearing shorts and a tank top, with drops of sweat glistening on her forehead. She'd never looked hotter. Antonia was taken aback when she realized Sánchez was eating the food she'd left for her.

Their eyes met, but neither of them spoke. Antonia took a bottled water out of the fridge, her shoulder grazing Sánchez when she walked. She waited for some kind of acknowledgment, but she got nothing except for a few furtive glances.

The attitude confirmed what she'd assumed—Sánchez wasn't happy with her presence.

She was halfway to her room when her damn mouth got the best of her. "You like my cooking?"

"It's better than starving," Sánchez answered.

The dry tone should have deterred Antonia from attempting any further conversation, but it spurred her on. If they were going to share the same space for the foreseeable future, they needed to clear the air and at least act cordial. She would be the bigger person. Part of her was also curious why Sánchez had gone back to that attitude after they'd been getting along better.

"Look, I'm just going to get this out of the way for both of our sakes," Antonia said, returning to the kitchen. "I don't know why you're back to hating me, but we're roommates now and things will be a lot better if we get along." At Sánchez's silence, she continued. "I thought we had something good going on."

Sánchez let out a long sigh. "That was before they forced me to live with you. We only got along briefly because we were sleeping together, but we can't do that now that we live together."

"Why not?"

"'Cause it's weird!" Sánchez exclaimed.

Antonia raised her eyebrows. "How is it any different from before?"

"It's not the same as sleeping with each other in hotel rooms or when you go back to your own place afterward. Sleeping together and sharing an apartment is just too . . . intimate."

Antonia took a sip of water to give herself time to process Sánchez's logic. "Okay. I don't get it, but if that's the issue, then we stop sleeping together. That doesn't mean you have to go back to being an asshole to me."

Sánchez replied to her words with an angry stare, but Antonia wouldn't let that stop her from fixing their situation once and for all. "I'm not asking you to be my best friend. Just . . . Let's give each other a chance to get along, even without the sex."

"Fine. I guess it's not your fault the team stuck us together." Sánchez took a bite of her food. "If you plan on cooking often, I may be able to stand you," she added. Her eyes softened, giving Antonia a glimmer of hope that they might be able to get along.

"That could be arranged, yeah."

The logical next step was for Antonia to leave now that they'd cleared the air, get into the shower to wash away the sweat from running. But she stood there, rooted to the spot, lost in Sánchez's eyes. And Sánchez seemed as lost as she was. The silence hung heavy between them, but neither dared to move, nor to speak.

Her eyes moved to Sánchez's lips right in time to catch the slow movement of her tongue over her dry mouth. Antonia cleared her throat and looked away before she ruined the tentative peace they'd established.

"I'm going to take a shower . . . See you later."

She could have sworn Sánchez looked disappointed.

In the shower, Antonia let the cold water soothe her aching muscles, but it did nothing to wash away her not-so-friendly thoughts about Sánchez.

Chapter Eleven

CAMILA HAD NEVER BEEN good at sharing her space. Maybe being an only child had something to do with it. She didn't know. But the fact was, she'd never been good at sharing, be it a space, things, or people. Even while playing, she sometimes was more selfish than she should be when what mattered was the team. Yet her annoyance with Antonia went beyond that. She didn't like the pull the other girl had on her. The way she lost control when it came to her.

She'd already failed at staying away from Antonia, failed at not getting involved with her. It had been hard enough to resist that pull when they only saw each other at training and matches. She could only imagine how hard it was going to be to keep her distance while they shared an apartment. It wasn't like she could share all that, though, so being mean seemed like the best course of action. Understandably, Antonia wasn't having it.

Camila hated to admit that Antonia was right, but spending all her time angry and on guard even in her own home, wasn't sustainable. She figured she may as well give the whole friendly approach a try. Maybe once she knew her better, once she found pieces of her long, curly hair clogging the shower drain and discovered all her annoying habits, the hold Antonia had over her would disappear.

She hoped that happened soon, because watching her walk out of the bathroom wrapped in a tiny towel wasn't helping her intentions. The shorts and tank tops Antonia wore around the house didn't help either. Or the way she stood by the door of her room, leaning against the wall.

"Do you mind if I join you?" Antonia asked.

If Camila didn't know better, she would've sworn the other girl even sounded shy. She shrugged, faking a nonchalance she didn't feel and hoping the loud, accelerated beating of her heart was impossible for Antonia to hear. "Sure."

The couch was simultaneously too big and too small for the both of them. Antonia sat in the opposite corner, giving Camila plenty of space. It should be what she wanted, but it wasn't. She longed for the heat of Antonia's body to be closer to her own. She wanted to breathe in the coconut-scented soap that still lingered on Antonia's skin. She fought the urge to grasp the back of her neck and pull her down on that couch.

Antonia's presence, even with the small physical distance between them, became intoxicating. Camila took a deep breath and inhaled Antonia's essence, let it fill her lungs and her chest, her heart and her soul. She felt warm from Antonia's closeness, from the way she filled the space even without trying. But on the outside, Camila tried her best to remain stoic. She stared ahead at the TV, pretending, hoping that maybe if she didn't look at her, Antonia's presence would stop putting her on edge.

"You know, I think we should have some ground rules," Camila blurted.

Antonia stopped chewing the food she was eating. "Like what?"

Camila had no idea, but she needed some kind of boundary. Anything to force herself to not do something stupid, like believing that she and Antonia could become more than rivals.

"Well, no bringing home strangers, no random hookups. You go to their place instead."

Antonia raised her eyebrows and smirked. "That should be no problem. I'm not in the habit of picking up strangers."

JOHANA GAVEZ

Camila scoffed. "Could have fooled me."

"I mean, technically, we knew each other," Antonia said, her smile growing bigger. "I didn't pick you up on the street."

"Barely," Camila mumbled.

The expression on Antonia's face was now a permanent fixture. One that unnerved Camila to no end. What was she smirking at? Why did she act as if she was privy to a secret no one else knew? If Antonia thought for one second that her request was because she was jealous or something ridiculous like that, she was sorely mistaken. Camila didn't like strangers in her space, that was all. It was bad enough she already had to share one with Antonia.

"Well, contrary to what you may think, I'm not looking for casual relationships. But sure, I'll have that rule in mind in case it's necessary. Anything else?"

Camila ignored the way her heart jumped at Antonia's words. "Yeah, a couple more things," she said to gain time while she struggled to come up with any other rules. She didn't want Antonia to think she was only interested in policing her relationships. "Food."

"Food?"

"Yeah. I've had issues in the past with roommates who ate all my groceries but never contributed."

"Okay . . . We can label them, I guess."

"I don't think that'll be necessary. I was thinking we could both chip in grocery money, and since it seems like you enjoy cooking, I'm happy to pay a little more for ingredients if you're going to cook."

Antonia shrugged. "That's fine."

"That's all, I think. Unless you want to add something?"

"No, I'm good. I've never been one for rules," Antonia answered with a wink that made Camila blush, even if she wasn't sure what was meant by it. "Actually, you know what," she added, "this is not a rule but a request."

"Go on."

"It's the last day of preseason. The last day we'll have to relax a little. So, what do you say we go out and do something fun?"

Alarm bells went off in Camila's brain. She was trying to stay away from Antonia, not spend more time with her. "You can go out and have fun, sure."

"Well, you know I still don't know how to get around the city, so that's where you come in."

Camila pushed aside the disappointment that it wasn't because Antonia wanted her company but that she needed a tour guide. "I don't know that much more than you, but I guess we could drive to Galveston or go to the Galleria."

"Galveston? That's the beach, right? I love the beach. Let's go!"

Fifteen minutes later, Camila was driving toward Galveston with a singing Antonia in the passenger seat. She didn't particularly like the song, and Antonia's voice wasn't in tune, but Camila found a smile tugging at the corners of her lips despite her best efforts.

It felt like déjà vu. Like a loop where she always ended up trapped somewhere with Antonia. She needed to find a way to stop ending up in that situation. At least this time she didn't have to interact with Antonia thanks to a perfectly timed phone call. Antonia babbled away without a care in the world, as if Camila wasn't even there the entire ride.

Antonia was loud and expressive while she spoke on the phone. Camila didn't understand a word, but she often sneaked a glance when Antonia laughed or when she moved her hands around, drawing a scene with wild movements as if the person on the other end of the line could see her.

"Estou com saudades de você," Antonia said, and she hung up right as they arrived in Galveston. It was staggering to see the sudden change in demeanor. How Antonia's voice dropped lower and all the exuberance left her.

She hadn't known Antonia for long, but Camila always felt as though she had her pegged. Confident, easygoing, loud. She looked so different, so small, hunched down in her seat, cradling the phone in her hands as she might a baby.

"Miss your girlfriend back in Brazil?" Camila joked, but she cringed as soon as she said it. "Sorry," she mumbled.

"I miss my brother. He's the only person I have."

"What does what you said at the end mean?" Camila asked. Even if she didn't understand the words, the longing in Antonia's voice was so raw, she almost felt it herself.

"Saudades?"

Camila nodded.

"It's hard to explain." She turned the phone over to show Camila the screen, and a picture of her with a handsome sandy-haired guy appeared in the background. "It means 'I miss you,' but also so much more than that." She looked away for a second before meeting her eyes again. "It means there's a hole in my chest, in my heart. That there's a part of my soul missing because it stayed back in Brazil with my brother. It means a longing I can never fill. We go through life leaving parts of us behind. That's not bad, it's part of living. But sometimes we miss those things, the people, the moments we've left behind, and we feel saudades. We feel a craving for what is no longer there." Antonia chuckled, seemingly back to her usual self, but the glint in her eyes was still missing. "Does that make sense?"

Camila stared at her for a long moment, wondering if this was the same girl she'd interacted with for the past couple of weeks. Maybe there was more to her than what she'd assumed. "I'm not sure," she breathed out in an almost whisper. "But it was beautiful."

Camila hadn't even finished parking the car before Antonia was already opening the door and running to the beach. The change in demeanor happened in a split second—from sad and contemplative to her usual effervescent self. Camila rolled her eyes, but as she watched Antonia skip toward the sand, a small smile tugged at the corners of her lips.

She walked slowly in the same direction until she caught up to Antonia, who had taken off her shoes and stood on the edge of the beach, staring ahead.

Camila watched Antonia, who seemed lost in her own thoughts, her gaze fixed in the distance. Camila basked in the curve of Antonia's jaw, followed the up-and-down movements of her chest as she took deep breaths of the salty air. She was aware she was staring but found herself unable to look away. Antonia looked so calm, so peaceful. She'd never seen her like that before.

She stood next to Antonia without saying a word for what felt like an eternity. She watched her close her eyes and open her arms wide as if trying to absorb the rough wind into her body. The longer they stood side by side, the harder it was for Camila to ignore the heat coming from Antonia. She knew it was ridiculous to feel so unnerved by the mere existence of another person, but she fought against the urge to take a step to the side to create some distance. Antonia was like a planet pulling her closer without even realizing. The only reason she didn't move was for fear of Antonia noticing the effect she had.

Antonia opened her eyes and took one last deep breath. "This is the saddest beach I've ever seen in my life."

Camila chuckled. "You're the one who wanted to come to the beach. I was happy staying home."

"I would have been happy to stay there too, if you had told me the beach looked like . . . this." Antonia waved her arms around.

Camila agreed that the gray—or kind of greenish brown—water in Galveston wasn't the most appealing. But Antonia only said she wanted to go out, and Camila obliged. She wasn't about to take responsibility for trying to help her.

"Let's go back, then."

"It was an observation, not a complaint," Antonia said, taking Camila's hand. "We're here already. Let's enjoy it."

Camila had no time to react. Antonia pulled her toward the water with a resounding laugh. Camila let out a yelp but didn't resist. It was too late to fight Antonia's enthusiasm, and for once she didn't want to. She smiled and laughed alongside her as they ran around, letting the waves hit their feet.

Antonia splashed the shallow water around in every direction while Camila stood next to her and watched. Antonia ran and kicked, jumped, and ran again, without a care in the world, until one particularly strong kick sent a splash of water toward Camila's face, drenching her from head to toe. They both froze in place, staring at each other. Antonia stood still with a horrified look on her face, as if only then realizing what she'd done and fearing the reaction. Camila, stunned by the coldness of the water, took in the worried expression on Antonia's face, which made her burst out laughing. At first it was only one low giggle, but soon another followed, and another, until she was overcome by an uncontrollable fit of laughter.

Antonia cocked her head to the side and squinted. Camila would've been confused, too, if their roles were reversed. Camila used the moment to return the splash of water, and the way it hit Antonia squarely in the face could not have been more perfect. It made her laugh louder, and this time Antonia joined in.

They sat on the beach after a while, exhausted after so much running. They were silent, both staring at the horizon like they'd done earlier. But this time, the silence didn't unnerve Camila, nor did the way their shoulders leaned into each other for support.

"So the beach wasn't so bad after all, huh?"

Antonia turned to look at her with soft eyes. "It did what it needed to do. Won't beat my beach, though."

"What's so special about your beach?" Camila asked, bumping Antonia's shoulder with hers.

"I don't know," Antonia replied. "It feels like home, I guess. This one is too quiet," she added, almost in a whisper.

Camila was about to reply when Antonia spoke again, although it seemed more like she was mumbling to herself rather than talking to Camila.

"There aren't even any kids playing football."

There was something endearing about Antonia in that moment. Something that made Camila want to see more of this side of her.

"I have a soccer ball in the car," she said, and the way Antonia's eyes lit up was all Camila needed to see in order to know that the softer side of Antonia was dangerous for her.

The urge to lean down for a kiss was strong, but Camila forced herself to look away. Having casual sex with Antonia was bad enough—letting herself consider falling for her was out of the question.

Retrieving the ball from her car was the perfect excuse to put some distance between them. When Camila got back to the beach, she watched Antonia from afar. She gave herself permission to stare, only for a minute, knowing she didn't have to worry about Antonia or anyone else noticing.

Antonia looked so innocent, so young. They were only two years apart, but Camila felt so much older. She couldn't remember the last time she spent a day without feeling a weight on her shoulders. Relaxing wasn't an option when you wanted to be the best—when you had to be the best. This trip to the beach with Antonia was already an outlier.

She was still standing with the ball in her hands when Antonia turned around and waved at her. Startled, Camila hit the ball in her direction to hide the fact that she'd been staring, even though Antonia didn't seem to notice or care. Her focus shifted to kicking the ball.

Camila walked toward her, a hint of jealousy rising up at how effortlessly she dominated the ball. She frowned when Antonia started running in her direction, only to have to react with lightning speed when the ball returned to her, thanks to an impeccable pass.

"Come on!" Antonia yelled, running backward and waving her hands in the air.

Camila rolled her eyes at her enthusiasm but hit the ball back.

"I thought you enjoyed playing football. Can't tell from the way you kicked that ball," Antonia added with a teasing smile.

"I wasn't expecting our day off to turn into work."

Antonia laughed. "We're not working, we're playing," she said, and kicked the ball back.

Camila let out a sigh before running to catch up with her. They began passing the ball back and forth along the beach. Despite her best efforts, she enjoyed the impromptu game, even when Antonia hogged the ball to show off her drill skills.

Camila ended the game by catching the ball. The sun was setting, and she had a feeling Antonia could play all day and night if she let her.

They walked back to the car in silence, but Antonia's pensive expression piqued Camila's interest.

"Penny for your thoughts?"

"What?" Antonia answered with the most adorable and confused look on her face.

"What are you thinking about?" Camila tried instead.

"My brother. I used to play with him on the beach, just like that," Antonia answered. A sad smile morphed into a teasing grin. "Well, he would have never stopped like you did. We would have played until I said so."

Camila ignored her attempt at diverting the conversation. "You two seem close. I always wanted a brother or sister. It sounded cool to have a potential best friend built into your family." She looked down. "Not that being family guarantees anything. With my luck, if I had a brother, he would be a jerk."

"My brother is everything to me. He always took care of me, and after my mom died, he sacrificed everything so I could make my dream a reality. I wouldn't be here if it wasn't for him dropping out of school and quitting the third-division team he played in so he could work and support me."

Camila realized there was so much more to Antonia than what she'd seen so far. She'd just started the car when Antonia spoke again.

"It's okay because I'm here now and all his sacrifices will be worth it. I'm going to help him open his own restaurant one day."

Camila nodded. There was no doubt in her mind that Antonia could do anything she set her mind to. She also felt a hint of shame that her own motivation for succeeding was so banal comparatively. She wanted to show the world that she was a good player who could become successful on her own, not because of her dad's help. Making him proud didn't sound as compelling as it usually did.

Chapter Twelve

ANTONIA WASN'T SURE IF she was making it up, but she could swear Sánchez was looking at her differently ever since their day at the beach. It was subtle, but it was there. The animosity in her eyes was no longer present, and they were almost getting along. At least at home, she no longer groaned or rolled her eyes when Antonia sat next to her to watch TV or cooked something for her. But they were back at training now, and in front of the coach, Sánchez became someone else. They were on opposite teams for this session, and the way Sánchez shoved her to rob the ball was completely unnecessary, in her opinion.

Antonia stood up, dusted herself off, and ran to catch up to her teammates. She'd let it go this time. She had to admit Sánchez was good, too. Having stolen the ball, Sánchez passed the ball and immediately took off running to gain the position inside the penalty area, between two defenders. When the high pass made it to them, they didn't reach fast enough. Sánchez was already in the air, heading the ball into the corner of the net.

She wasn't as skilled as Antonia. It wasn't arrogance for her to think that—it was just a fact. But Sánchez compensated with grit and strength. If the coach gave her a chance, Antonia was sure they would make a great duo.

The smirk taking over Sánchez's face after the goal reminded Antonia of their brief encounters. It was that confidence, that tinge of conceit, that both infuriated her and drew her to Sánchez at the same time.

When Antonia moved her eyes away from Sánchez's fit, muscular body, her team was already in position to restart play. She ran to the sideline, moving to her favorite area to lead the attack, but her teammates quickly lost the ball.

It was back and forth until almost the end of practice. The defenders on her side obstructed one clear attack and threw a long pass toward her to surprise with a counterattack. Antonia wasted no time running as fast as she could in the opposite direction. She knew nobody on the team could match her speed, so after disposing of the lone defender who had stayed behind, it was only her against the goalkeeper.

She had many options to score, and she was sure she wouldn't fail, no matter which one she chose. But of course, she went for the most spectacular one. What was the fun of playing it safe? She watched as the goalkeeper moved forward to close her shooting angle, but instead of shooting before she got near, she waited. At the last possible moment, she stepped on the ball with her left foot, made a 180-degree turn, and pulled the ball toward her with a precise movement of her feet, away from the goalkeeper, who was already splayed on the grass and unable to catch her. With the goal fully open and unopposed in front of her, it was only a matter of pushing the ball softly past the goal line.

She celebrated with her practice teammates first, before sneaking a glance in Sánchez's direction. She was scowling, but when their eyes met, she shook her head and rolled her eyes with a small smile on her face. Antonia returned the smile and winked at her.

Antonia was the last one to make it to the locker room. She'd asked the coach for permission to stay later to practice her free kicks, so she remained on the pitch for almost an hour, honing her skills and trying her best to place the ball in the top-right corner of the goal. She'd always had perfect aim, but only with practicing the same shot over and over again could she increase her chances of being close to scoring every time she took a free kick in a game.

When she opened the door to the locker room, Sánchez was sitting on the bench, scrolling on her phone. There were a couple of other girls around, but they were leaving.

"Did you wait for me?" Antonia asked in a teasing tone.

"Of course not," Sánchez scoffed. "You're lucky everyone hogged the showers so it took me forever to get ready."

Antonia pretended to not notice the way Sánchez avoided her eyes. "Well, I don't want to keep you waiting, so I'll take an Uber if you need to leave now."

She was halfway to the showers when Sánchez's voice stopped her.

"Since I'm still here, I can wait for you—if you don't take forever."

The corners of Antonia's lips rose in a smile, but she forced them back down. "I'll hurry, then."

Camila could hear the water running a few steps away, and knowing they were alone in the locker room, she couldn't help but picture herself walking into the shower, kissing Antonia's neck, pushing her against the cold tile, and letting her hands roam.

A knock on the door saved her from her own thoughts. She frowned, wondering who would knock instead of just entering. Camila opened the door to find her dad standing outside.

She joined him and closed the door behind her. "Hey. What are you doing here?"

"Hola, cariño. I have an important meeting with Franco. I won't stay long, but I couldn't leave without saying hi to you."

"You just flew in for the meeting?"

"Yeah, I landed like two hours ago, and I leave again tonight. You know how it is."

It wasn't unusual for her dad to travel for work. He was part of several company boards and committees for different soccer organizations, but flying all the way to Houston just to see her coach? Even if they were friends, it didn't make sense, but she kept her doubts to herself.

"It's great seeing you, even if only for a minute."

"I promise I'll make time to come see you soon." He cupped her cheek. "Maybe for your next match. I love to see you play."

She looked away from him. "You know I'm not on the starter team yet."

"I'm sure that'll change soon."

She didn't have a chance to ask him what he meant. He looked at his watch and leaned down to kiss her forehead.

"I have to go now, but I'll be back soon."

With one hand on the door of the locker room, Camila watched him walk away. Once he turned a corner, she took off after him. She moved slowly, giving him time to get ahead of her by waiting with her back to the wall and counting to one hundred in her head. She then followed the path she already knew to Coach Medina's office and stood outside his door, looking around to make sure nobody else was there.

"You didn't have to come all the way here just to threaten me," Coach Medina said.

The anger in his voice and the words themselves took Camila aback, but her dad seemed unfazed when he answered. "It's not a threat. Only a friendly reminder. There's a lot of things you owe me for, and I hope you don't forget about that."

Coach Medina scoffed. "You've become too used to using your influence to benefit yourself. That's going to be your downfall."

Camila didn't need to hear more. She didn't want to hear more. She retraced her steps in a trance, not even realizing where she was going. As she walked, her surprise turned into anger. They had to be talking about her. Her dad was trying to leverage his relationship with the coach for her, and she hated him for it.

When the first drops of hot water hit her aching muscles, Antonia resisted the urge to relax under the spray and let the liquid engulf her for hours. She was sure Sánchez wouldn't leave without her no matter how long she made her wait, but she didn't want to test her luck. Besides, seeing her expression when Antonia walked in wearing only a minuscule towel would be worth more than proving she was right about Sánchez choosing to wait for her.

Her plan was ruined when Sánchez was nowhere to be found once she got to the lockers. Had she left just to mess with her? Or was she waiting outside?

Sánchez opened the door a few minutes later with her jaw clenched and her eyebrows knitted in a deep frown. "Are you ready?" she snapped.

Antonia decided it wasn't the time to joke about how she'd missed the chance of seeing her naked again. "Yeah, I'm good to go."

"Good," Sánchez mumbled, and she walked away without waiting to see if Antonia followed her.

Antonia knew she should leave Sánchez alone. She knew it—but she didn't listen to herself.

"Is everything okay?"

"I'm fine."

It was clear in her tone that she didn't want to talk about whatever was bothering her. That didn't stop Antonia from asking again. "You seem pretty upset for someone who's fine."

Sánchez let out a sigh. "I was walking around while I waited for you and saw my dad talking to Coach Medina."

Antonia was surprised she'd gotten an answer, but she still didn't understand why Sánchez was upset. "Why is that bad?"

"They've been friends for a long time, and last week I complained to my dad about how the coach wasn't planning on having me as a starter. He was probably trying to call in a favor to make him give me a spot on the team. It's what he does."

Antonia's jaw dropped. She was at a loss for words, but she didn't have to provide any. Now that Sánchez had started talking, she was on a roll.

"He always pulls the same shit, no matter how much I ask him not to. I know I'm an excellent player. I don't need him using his influence to help me."

They drove the rest of the way to their apartment in silence. Sánchez made a beeline for her bedroom as soon as they were inside, but Antonia grabbed her hand to stop her. She'd been thinking about what to say, and she still didn't know. But she knew she couldn't let Sánchez go to bed without saying something.

"You're a great player," she whispered, trying to show Sánchez just how much she meant it.

A shift in weight woke Antonia. It took her a second to realize that Sánchez was sitting at the end of her bed. She looked at her through hazy eyes. Was she dreaming? Sánchez had too many clothes on, compared to her usual dreams. The way Sánchez avoided her eyes confirmed she was intruding in her room like a sexy ghost.

Antonia rubbed her eyes and stifled a yawn. "Hey," she said.

Sánchez didn't answer but started to climb up on the bed until she was lying by Antonia's side. She raised a hand to cup Antonia's face with a softness they'd never used before. Antonia wanted to ask her what was happening, but the vulnerability in Sánchez's movements told her it was better to remain silent and still until Sánchez got what was bothering her out of her system.

"I can't sleep."

It didn't explain why she was in this bed, but Antonia nodded anyway, as if it made sense. Sánchez's palm warmed her cheek—a warmth that spread from Antonia's face to her chest and belly. It was soft and calming, and it only increased when Sánchez's thumb traveled to caress her mouth.

"I just want my mind to go blank, and I couldn't think of any other way but you," Sánchez whispered.

Antonia had no time to process the words because soft lips immediately touched her own, and her mind also went blank.

An annoying voice in the back of her head told her she should stop. It was obvious that Sánchez wasn't okay, and the fact that she'd climbed into Antonia's bed in the middle of the night only proved it. Even more worrying was that they weren't kissing with the usual roughness and desperation they usually shared. The kiss increased in pace and intensity, but it remained soft in a way Antonia wasn't used to. She could have been able to ignore all that, maybe, if she hadn't tasted the remnants of a tear on Sánchez's lips.

Antonia moved away only an inch, barely enough to create distance between them without startling

Sánchez. "Are you sure this is what you need?" she asked, wiping tears from Sánchez's face.

Sánchez closed her eyes. "Please, I can't deal with you rejecting me right now."

"I don't want to reject you. I just want to make sure you're not doing something you'll regret."

"I'm not. Please, I need to feel wanted."

Antonia leaned down and sucked on Sánchez's bottom lip. "I want you," she breathed out, and she went back in for a deeper kiss.

She wasn't sure if she could give Sánchez what she craved, what she so desperately sought. But she was going to try.

She forgot about herself and focused only on making Sánchez feel better. She moved down Sánchez's body, removing the few pieces of clothes in her way—the tank top first, then the shorts, then the black panties. She slid those down, marveling at sculpted calves as she finished taking them off.

It was about Sánchez, Antonia told herself again. But she couldn't deny that she enjoyed the chance to worship her slowly. Softer than she had before. She kissed knees on the way up. She planted a trail of kisses from stomach to her chest, then stopped to look into Sánchez's eyes before claiming her lips again.

After the kiss ended, their eyes met once more, and this time Antonia got lost in the hazel pools looking

JOHANA GAVEZ

back at her with unshed tears. The raw emotion panged her heart, and something rose within her—an unstoppable desire to protect Sánchez, to shield her from the pain she was feeling. She brought one of her hands up to caress Sánchez's face, and to her surprise, the other girl leaned into the touch.

They didn't exchange any words, but Antonia swore there was an understanding between them, a silent communication. Sánchez asked her to catch her as she fell, and Antonia showed her she would, even if only for one night.

"Please," Sánchez whispered.

Antonia nodded and planted a peck on the corner of Sánchez's left eye, and then she moved to the other side to do the same. As her hand traveled south, she let her body rest on top until their foreheads touched.

Wetness engulfed her fingers, and she paused for only a second to bask in the sensation before entering Sánchez with a skilled touch. She never stopped looking at Sánchez, and even after the other girl closed her eyes, Antonia drank her in. She marveled at the expressions on Sánchez's face, mouth open in a never-ending moan, the small frown, and the drop of sweat sliding down.

She kept pleasuring Sánchez, encouraged by her moans, by the way she grasped at her back and wrapped one leg around her waist as if trying to bring her closer, deeper. And then she held on while Sánchez opened her eyes to stare back at her with a glazed expression.

"Thank you," Sánchez breathed. One second later, she buried her head into the crook of Antonia's neck.

Antonia held her tight and covered them with the displaced sheet as the clock on her nightstand marked the early morning.

Camila woke up wrapped around Antonia's body, and her instinct was to stay in her warm embrace. But she didn't. She'd already broken all her boundaries by seeking her in the middle of the night. There was no point in getting comfortable when she knew it couldn't happen again. It was embarrassing enough that she'd begged Antonia to take her. She wouldn't stay around to have the other girl tell her it had been a pity fuck and nothing more. She wanted to keep what was left of her dignity intact.

At least it had helped her forget the fact that, as usual, her dad was using his influence to advance her career because he didn't believe in her. Because she would never be enough in his eyes. When Antonia touched her the night before, she forgot about everything. She felt wanted and desired. She felt, for once, that she was enough.

Yet she knew it was all an illusion.

Antonia didn't want her beyond the occasional night of passion. Not that she wanted to have a relationship with her. Of course not. Though it would be nice to be someone's top choice for once.

Sleeping with Antonia was what she had needed the night before. But it was another day, and now what she needed was to forget she had exposed herself so much.

Camila extracted herself from Antonia's embrace and ran to the shower to wash away the memories of the day before. It would be pointless to get used to the situation when it would never happen again.

She spent longer than normal in the shower, letting the hot water erase the last remnants of her sweat and tears. Once she stepped out, there would be no more crying. She would stick to that decision. It hurt to be reminded of how little her dad thought of her, and she had no other choice but to keep going. Keep trying to show her worth.

As usual, Antonia was in the kitchen when Camila got out of the bathroom. Thankfully, she was focused on whatever she was cooking on the stove and didn't stop her on the way to her room. Or maybe she pretended to not notice her because she knew the last thing

Camila wanted was to talk. No matter the reason, she was grateful for the respite.

Her initial plan was to avoid Antonia, but the smell of bacon was too much for her to handle on an empty stomach. She chose to not dwell on the fact that she was sure there would be a plate waiting for her at the kitchen bar.

Antonia was biting a piece of pound cake and drinking her coffee when Camila joined her. As expected, a plate with fruit, eggs, and bacon waited for her. The way Antonia looked at her with a mix of curiosity and wonder was unnerving. It made Camila want to run back inside her room to stop feeling exposed, but it was too late now. She doubted she was hiding her discomfort, but running away would be admitting it. Instead, she took a bite of her food. That way, at least she would have an excuse to not answer if Antonia decided to have a heart-to-heart.

"So, we don't have to talk about last night if you don't want to," Antonia said.

"You just talked about it," Camila replied with more edge to her voice than she intended.

Antonia smiled and took another sip of coffee. She was leaning down on the kitchen counter, and Camila thought she had no business looking that sexy and confident when they were in the middle of an awkward conversation.

"My bad. I will continue to not talk about it by telling you I'm here for you as a friend."

"We're not friends."

"I know." She smiled. "I'm still here for you, though."

The sincerity in Antonia's eyes was too much for Camila to take, so she did the only thing she could. She looked down at her food and pretended to focus on cutting a piece of fruit as though it was the hardest task she'd ever had to do.

"I'm going to shower," Antonia said, walking toward her bedroom. "Don't leave without me!"

After what felt like an eternity, Camila spoke to the empty room. "Thank you."

The sound of the bathroom door opening startled her, and she turned around.

Antonia poked her head through the half-opened door with a smile. "You're welcome."

Chapter Thirteen

AS MUCH AS CAMILA tried to forget about seeing her dad talking in hushed tones with her coach, she couldn't. It was even harder to shake it from her mind when Coach Medina announced the lineup for their away game against the Orlando Ducks. For the first time that season, she was on the starting team as a central forward.

Liz hugged her after the announcement. "See, I told you the coach would realize how good you are," she exclaimed in her ear.

"Yeah," Camila mumbled back, barely able to fake excitement.

Antonia also congratulated her by smacking her ass. "Don't worry. It'll be easy for you to score with the amazing passes I always make."

Rolling her eyes at Antonia almost made Camila forget the reason for her lack of enthusiasm.

Part of her wanted to confront Coach Medina, to ask him if her dad was the only reason she would play that day. But she didn't. She didn't know how the coach would react to being confronted, and maybe she was afraid to confirm that her fears were true. It was one thing to assume that's what her dad had been doing that night, and another to have it confirmed without a sliver of doubt left. If she was honest with herself, there was also another reason she didn't talk to him—she wanted to play.

She knew it was hypocritical of her to claim she didn't want her dad's help and then turn around and take advantage of it. But she wanted to play, and if this was her only chance, she was going to show she had earned it.

When they stepped onto the field, the only thing on her mind was to show everyone she deserved to be there. Antonia, true to her word, served her several deep passes that put her in a perfect position to score. She failed the first two by inches, but on the third try, she watched as Antonia controlled the ball after a long pass right outside the penalty area. When everybody expected her to shoot on goal, she stopped midmovement to pass the ball to Camila, who was diagonal from her. From there, Camila shot with precision and sent the ball to the back of the net.

Without thinking, she ran to Antonia and jumped into her outstretched arms. In that instant, Camila felt happy for the first time since she'd overheard her dad.

"Thanks for the pass," she said as Antonia was about to run away from her.

"I knew you wouldn't miss."

The rest of the game was a blur for Camila. Coach Medina pulled her out of the game at the seventy-minute mark, but nothing could erase her happiness. Her team scored another two goals for an overwhelming win. The entire time, there was only one thing on her mind: She wanted to celebrate with Antonia.

"We're celebrating tonight," Liz said to Camila when they got to the hotel. "And I won't hear your excuses. We're all meeting in an hour to go out. I'll drag you out of your room if you're not here."

Camila smiled. "I'm in the mood to celebrate. I'll be there."

She was glad she'd packed a little black dress. After putting on some light makeup and a pair of heels, she was ready for the night. Funnily enough, she was one of the first few to arrive in the lobby. She should have known Liz would never be ready in only an hour.

Of course, it was her luck that not five minutes later, Antonia stepped out of the elevator. She wore a simple white button-down, black jeans, and a pair of sneakers, but Camila thought she couldn't look sexier. There wasn't a drop of makeup on her face, and her long, curly hair hung over her shoulders. She'd never looked better, and Camila found it impossible to tear her gaze away.

"Hey there," Antonia said, coming closer. "You ready to party?"

Camila licked her lips as she stared at Antonia, forgetting that she was trying to hide how much she wanted her. "I am, but seems like nobody else is."

"They'll be here any minute. López texted me they were on their way down."

Camila was aware of Antonia's gaze, of the way she moved her eyes up and down Camila's body in an invisible caress that electrified her senses.

"You look good," Antonia said.

"Thank you. You clean up nicely too."

"This? You should see me in a suit." Antonia winked.

Camila let out a cough at the image. She pictured Antonia in a sharp three-piece suit, and if the real thing looked half as good as her imagination, she would be a goner if Antonia ever decided to wear one in front of her. Even worse was what her mind conjured up next: Antonia taking off the pieces of her suit until she was left only with an open shirt and a tie dangling between perky breasts.

López and Liz chose that moment to appear in front of her, pulling her out of her thoughts.

"The Uber is almost here," Liz said. "The rest of the team will meet us there."

In the car, Camila ended up pressed close to Antonia. Once again, she thanked all the gods that Antonia preferred pants to dresses. If their bare thighs had touched, Camila would've had to consider opening the car door and jumping into the open road to avoid the onslaught of feelings that Antonia's closeness caused. She still thought about doing it when she noticed the obvious goose bumps on her legs.

She was saved from certain death, thanks to the fact that Antonia was in an animated conversation with López.

"When are you and Young going to admit you're banging?" she heard Antonia say.

"It's not any of your business, but I'll tell you what. We will admit it when you and Sánchez stop dancing around each other and admit you're in love."

Camila's stomach leaped to her throat. She knew López was just trying to mess with Antonia, but the word "love" sent a shiver through her entire body.

"I've barely gotten Sánchez here to not bite my head off in the morning," Antonia answered without missing a beat. "We're still very far from love, but I'm getting there one cup of coffee at a time."

Antonia bumped Camila's shoulder. "Right, roomie?"

Camila begged her voice to not betray her, as her warm cheeks already had. "I can stand her now."

"See, she can stand me. That's almost as good as love," Antonia replied with a chuckle. "Don't think I didn't notice how you diverted attention from my question. I'll keep my eye on you all night."

Camila let out a scoff that made everyone turn to look at her. "You're ridiculous," she said, but the retort lacked her usual sharpness. Instead it was soft, and she smiled when she said it. When three pairs of eyes stared at her in different states of confusion, she cleared her throat and added, "Why wouldn't they tell us if they're together? We'd all be happy for them."

"That's what I said!" Antonia exclaimed, turning to look pointedly at López.

Camila watched her, and while she did, all the sounds faded away. Antonia's boisterous laugh and López's annoyed groans became a distant echo she barely perceived. She kept looking at Antonia and wondering what it was about her that lowered all her defenses.

She could have spent the entire ride doing that if it weren't for Liz's questioning expression breaking her bubble. When she realized her friend was watching her, she spun her head toward the window and focused on the cars whizzing by instead—to avoid Liz's stare, to distract from Antonia's closeness, and to escape her own thoughts.

Antonia noticed the obvious way Sánchez looked at her. What she didn't know was what to do about it. Should she call her out on it? She was growing tired of the erratic dance they had going on, of feeling like they'd taken a step forward in their . . . friendship? Relationship? Whatever it was they had, only to find Sánchez running in the opposite direction soon after.

She didn't care about labels. If they kept their casual sex arrangement, she wouldn't hate it, but if Sánchez only wanted to be friends, she was also okay with that. The problem was the contradictions. The way Sánchez told her one thing in the morning and then crawled into her bed at night anyway. Antonia knew she would never reject Sánchez when she sought comfort, but she also knew that if they didn't talk about it or stick to what they'd agreed on, the risk of things getting out of hand increased. But with the beats of electronic music pounding around her and Sánchez looking exquisite in that black dress, the last thing Antonia wanted to do was talk.

She got up from her spot at the bar and joined the circle of dancing teammates, inserting herself right next to the woman who occupied her thoughts. As she expected, the group eventually broke up, and Antonia ended up alone with Sánchez, who did her best to pretend the closeness didn't affect her.

"Are you following me?" Sánchez said, backing away from her.

"I'm dancing."

"And it has to be right next to me?"

Antonia tilted her head. She had a feeling Sánchez didn't want her to go away, that her reaction was more out of habit, to save face, than out of a genuine desire to keep her at a distance.

"I enjoy dancing with you, but I'll go somewhere else if that's what you want," Antonia said, taking a tentative step back.

"You can stay." Sánchez shrugged. "I only wanted to gauge your intentions."

Someone bumped into Antonia, pushing her closer to Sánchez. "I thought I'd been clear about my intentions." She paused, enjoying the way Sánchez was trying hard to appear unaffected, but her fidgety eyes gave her away. "I'll follow your lead. If you tell me to stay away, I'll stay away, but I don't see why we can't be friendly."

When Sánchez said nothing back, Antonia moved another step closer. Close enough she could place her mouth right next to Sánchez's ear. "I enjoy your company, even when we're not . . . you know."

She moved away, stopping only when her eyes met Sánchez's. They were so close already, and they got pushed even closer by the people moving around them to the beat of the music. Antonia rested her hand on Sánchez's waist, the tips of her fingers touching the soft fabric of her dress.

"I need to pee," Sánchez announced. She turned away without another word and pushed her way through the mass of bodies, leaving a stunned Antonia behind.

The line to the restroom was massive and moved slowly, but Camila didn't mind. It gave her more time away from Antonia. She had to pee, but putting distance between the two of them was her primary motivation for staying in the line.

Things would be much easier if Antonia didn't look so good, if she didn't insist on being nice to her, if she didn't flash that bright smile of hers anytime they talked. It would be so easy to fall back into her arms. When she had Antonia close, filling her senses with her intoxicating coconut smell and the warm tingles of her breath in her ear, Camila forgot why she insisted on staying away.

That's why she needed to run away to the bathroom: to stop herself before she surrendered to Antonia's charms again. No matter how good it felt in the moment—and Camila knew from experience that it felt amazing—she didn't want more complications in her life. Having to deal with her dad's meddling exhausted all her emotional reserves. She didn't want to focus on second-guessing her interactions with Antonia. Keeping her at arm's length was the easiest way to accomplish that.

She took her phone out to pass the time, as the line had barely moved in the last ten minutes. A text message from her dad waited for her.

Hey, princess. You played amazing today.

Despite everything, the message filled her heart. The one thing she'd always wanted was to make her dad proud.

Thank you! I wanted to make the most out of my chance. I'm still not a shoo-in to start every game, and I want to change that.

Don't worry, I'm sure you won't be on the bench any longer. I'll talk to your mom about visiting you soon. Love you, cariño.

The air left her lungs, and a sinking feeling settled in her stomach. There was only one reason he could be sure about her prospects on the team. Once again, he had intervened on her behalf. As if she needed more confirmation. Maybe she should have stayed on the dance floor with Antonia. At least with her, she could forget about all her inadequacies. Antonia was good at that.

As if on cue, Antonia rounded the corner to join her in the restroom line. "Too much rum and Coke," she said with a sheepish grin.

Camila barely let Antonia finish speaking before grabbing her by the lapels of her shirt and pulling her in for a messy kiss. Their lips collided hard against each other, and she felt a sharp twinge of pain from where her eager lips hit Antonia's teeth. But the pain dissipated, and Antonia also adapted fast. Soon her lips were moving against Camila's just as enthusiastically.

Before she knew it, her back was firmly pressed against the wall, and Antonia was as close as she could be. The fast rumble of the electronic music seemed to fall in perfect sync with the movements of their lips.

She was aware of the people around her in the same way a camera registers an out-of-focus background. Part of her brain caught the sound of people hollering, but it was distant, barely perceptible. Most of her attention focused on Antonia's touch. Not only her lips, but the hand holding on to her waist, the way their legs rubbed against each other. Most of all, she was aware of the increasing wetness soaking her underwear and the desire building inside her.

If it were up to her, they'd have never stopped kissing, but Antonia eventually broke their connection. She didn't move away, staying almost in the same position except for the inches separating their lips.

"I'm not complaining, but where did that come from?" Antonia asked.

Camila wished Antonia would go back to kissing her instead, but she knew this was Antonia's way of checking again that this was what she wanted.

"I felt like it," she whispered against Antonia's open mouth, and she grabbed her lower lip between her teeth.

Antonia considered if she should push Sánchez on her answer. In the space of half an hour, she'd gone from avoiding her, to the point of running to the restroom to get away, to kissing her senseless. She couldn't think of any reason for the change, but it was suspicious. She knew that if she pressed, Sánchez would shut her down and she would risk ruining the moment. A packed and noisy club was not the best place to have deep conversations either.

"I shouldn't tempt my luck by asking if something's up?"

"Yeah, I think you shouldn't," Sánchez replied, pulling Antonia closer by the back of her neck.

It was hard to focus with Sánchez's lips attached to hers. Pretty much all thoughts left her mind the moment Sánchez sucked her lower lip and then teased her mouth with her tongue.

Her hand wandered, moving from its resting place on Sánchez's waist down her thighs until she reached soft skin. Sánchez didn't object. If anything, her kisses increased in intensity. That emboldened Antonia enough to keep moving her hand, this time inching it toward Sánchez's back to grab her ass and bring their bodies closer.

She moved away when her need for air overcame her need for Sánchez, but she didn't intend to stay away from her lips for long. The plan was to dive back in, until an exasperated girl next to them interrupted them.

"I'm about to piss myself, so either use the restroom or move your make-out session out of the way."

Sánchez chuckled. "Sorry, go ahead." She took Antonia's hand and walked back to the bar.

"Hey, what if I needed to go?"

"Come on, we both know you followed me 'cause spending ten minutes apart was too much for you."

"Oh, that's what you think?" Antonia answered. "What about you? It seemed like you really needed to go when you ran away from me."

Sánchez mimicked the smirk on Antonia's face. "I guess my need to pee went away."

Antonia ignored the flutter in her heart at seeing Sánchez so relaxed and joking back at her, but she didn't stop smiling or looking at her until they reached the table where the rest of their teammates waited for them.

"Where are López and Liz?" Brown asked. "We're ready to go, but we can't find them anywhere."

Antonia glanced at Sánchez, and they both shrugged at the same time. Since they'd shared a ride on the way there, it made sense that the responsibility of finding their missing teammates fell on them.

"We'll stay behind and look for them," Antonia assured the group.

Five minutes later, the rest of the team was on their way back to the hotel while Sánchez and Antonia walked around the club trying to find López and Young.

"Where the hell are they?" Sánchez asked after their third walk-around.

"Probably making out in some corner. I'm jealous of them."

Sánchez rolled her eyes. "They're not dating. Liz would have told me."

"I never said they were dating. Making out and dating are not the same."

"Right," Sánchez mumbled.

Maybe Antonia imagined it, but she could swear there was a hint of disappointment in her voice.

"This place is gigantic. How are we ever going to find them?"

Antonia looked around. "Let's start with the dark corners."

Sánchez groaned but followed her lead. They made their way around the crowd, trying to catch a glimpse of López's black leather jacket or Young's signature ponytail.

"If we don't find them soon, I'm going to actually go pee this time," Sánchez muttered, annoyance clear in her tone.

Those words gave Antonia an idea. "How long were you in that bathroom line? Like fifteen minutes at least and it never moved, right?"

"Yeah, I think so," Sánchez replied without looking at her.

"I can't believe it didn't occur to me before. Come on."

She grabbed Sánchez's hand and didn't wait for an answer before heading straight for the restrooms. The line was as long as when they left, and she recognized some of the angry faces still waiting.

"I'm sorry. Excuse me." Antonia wiggled her way to the front of the line, hoping her hunch was right. She knocked as hard as possible on the door. "López, come on! Time to go."

After a long silence that made Antonia doubt herself, López's muffled voice called, "One minute."

Antonia couldn't resist the urge to give Sánchez a look that said "I told you so" when López and Young walked out of the bathroom.

"I had a wardrobe malfunction, and she was helping me," Young explained.

"Sure." Antonia grinned. "Everybody else left, and since we rode together, we didn't want to ditch you."

"Thanks. That's nice of you," López said.

"I'm sure you're eager to get to your hotel room, so let's go," Antonia added with a wink.

"Shut up," López warned.

As soon as they crammed themselves in an Uber again, all distractions stopped, and Antonia had no choice but to wonder what was going to happen once they got to the hotel. Her make-out session with Sánchez seemed so long ago, even though it had been barely half an hour, and it surprised her to realize that, for once, she was unsure about how to act next.

Chapter Fourteen

THE DING OF THE elevator rang in Camila's ears. While the doors closed, she had time to follow Liz and López with her eyes until they rounded the corner, walking in the same direction, even though Liz's room was the other way. She stood awkwardly in the elevator, unable to say anything to Antonia. She couldn't speak when she wasn't sure what she wanted to say.

Yes, kissing her felt amazing and had helped her forget her worries. Now that the moment had passed, the voice in the back of her mind that told her it was a bad idea was louder than ever.

"Good night," she said when the elevator stopped on her floor.

Part of her wished—hoped—Antonia would say something, anything, to change her mind.

"Good night," Antonia answered back.

Five minutes later, Camila lay awake in bed, wondering why she was alone when, with one word, she could've had Antonia there with her. The emptiness of the space weighed on her heavier than ever, almost suffocating her.

It would have been so easy to walk to Antonia's room, so easy to call her, or text her, and ask for her company. But the idea of once again making it clear how much she needed Antonia kept Camila in place. She'd already jumped her one time that night—doing it twice was too much. If Antonia wanted her, she could've said so. Instead, she let her walk away.

The next morning, she was up earlier than necessary thanks to the constant swirl of thoughts in her mind. For lack of something better to do, she went to the hotel restaurant to get breakfast. The twelve-dollar buffet would be a far cry from the home-cooked meals Antonia made her almost every day, but it would have to do.

As if she'd called her with her thoughts, the first thing Camila saw once she reached the restaurant was Antonia struggling with the waffle maker. She smiled to herself and walked over to her after picking up a plate.

"You need help with that?"

"They keep getting stuck and ruining the shape," Antonia said with an adorable pout.

"Grab a table and I'll take care of the waffles."

When she joined Antonia with a plate full of waffles shaped like Mickey Mouse, Antonia's eyes lit up.

"Here you go," Camila said. "You really are a big Disney fan."

"I guess," Antonia answered, putting an obscene amount of whipped cream on top of her waffles. "When I was a kid, it all looked so magical. My brother and I always said we would go to Disney World together when we grew up and had money." She let out a small laugh. "It sounds silly, but that dream was so far away, yet still attainable at the same time."

"It's cute," Camila replied. "And I'm sure you will get to do that soon."

A sad smile took over Antonia's face. "I don't know. He had his visa appointment last week, and they denied it. So who knows when I'll be able to bring him here."

"Oh, I'm sorry. That sucks." Camila drank a sip of her coffee. It tasted horrible. "Do you know why?"

"I mean, they don't give you a reason, but he is young, no wife or kids, not the best job. They probably think he would try to stay here permanently. I thought adding my information to the form would help, but it wasn't enough."

Camila tried to think of something to ease Antonia's sudden melancholy. She'd rarely shown herself to be anything but happy and full of energy. It was weird to see this side of her.

"Do you think he would be sad or happy for you if you went without him?" Camila asked, an idea forming in her mind.

"Oh, he would be thrilled. He would never be jealous or bitter."

"Well, we're in Orlando, so why not go to the parks? You can FaceTime with him and send him a million pictures."

Antonia's eyes sparkled, and Camila's heart melted.

"But we're leaving in a couple hours," Antonia said, suddenly deflating.

"The team is leaving. We can stay. We would need to book our own flight and ask the coach, but we could do it."

"I'd love to," Antonia said, and this time the wide smile lighting up her face never wavered.

"Okay. I'll talk to the coach while you finish breakfast."

Camila stood up, feeling energized. As she was about to leave, a hand on her arm stopped her.

"Thank you."

Antonia looked in every direction, drinking in the sights around her, unable to believe she was standing in the middle of Magic Kingdom. She stopped short in the middle of the street, trying to decide which way to go first when she wanted to experience everything.

She didn't react when someone bumped into her. She didn't pay attention to the hordes of kids running around. The only thing that broke the spell the park had cast upon her was the graze of Sánchez's fingers over her hand. She turned to look at her and saw a brightness in those eyes that she wasn't used to seeing.

Sánchez gripped her hand. "Do you want a picture with Mickey?"

Heat rose in Antonia's cheeks, but when she looked at Sánchez, she didn't seem to be mocking her. There was a soft smile on her face that made Antonia's heart skip a beat.

"Yeah, I do."

Sánchez pulled her toward a building to their right, and the butterflies Antonia had been feeling since they walked into the park fluttered in her stomach. She tried to ignore them. Force them to calm down. But anytime Sánchez looked at her, they came back stronger than before, doing somersaults and acrobatics up and down her rib cage. The last couple of days, things with Sánchez had gone from cold to hot and back to cold so many times she was afraid of how the day would end. If she was honest with herself, maybe what made her so nervous was the way spending time with Sánchez was becoming one of her favorite things in the world.

When the tips of her fingers brushed Sánchez's hand, a warm tingle went up her arm, all the way to her chest. As if Antonia needed more confirmation, that reaction made it more than clear that the reason for her nervousness had a name: Camila Sánchez.

The other girl being so nice to her confused Antonia, since until that point she'd barely tolerated her and had made clear she wanted nothing to do with her beyond the occasional night together. Antonia had no reason to complain, of course. She'd been more than happy with the arrangement, but no matter how much she'd tried to convince Sánchez of the merits of being friends before, now that they were establishing a tentative friendship, the reality of it was messing with her head.

"Are you excited?" Sánchez asked.

It took a second for Antonia to realize what she meant, since she'd been lost in her own thoughts. "Yeah, I'm so excited," she said with a wide smile, hoping Sánchez wouldn't notice she'd been distracted. "My brother once paid one of his friends to dress up as Mickey for my birthday. They got the cheapest costume they could find, and it didn't look like him at all." Antonia chuckled. "I loved it anyway, but it looked more like a pigeon than a mouse. I'm sure that won't be the case here."

Sánchez laughed. "That's cute, though. Your brother sounds great."

"He is," Antonia answered, turning to look at her.

She was met with a sea of hazel staring back at her. She'd seen Sánchez's eyes so many times before. She'd seen her scowl, and she'd also gotten lost in dilated pupils that darkened from hazel to brown, but never before had she seen this light in Sánchez's eyes. That glint of happiness. It suited her.

Antonia leaned in, like she was being pulled by an invisible string toward Sánchez. She was so close, seconds away from kissing her right there and then, when the line moved in front of them. Antonia recovered her senses enough to tear her eyes away from Sánchez's face.

The line was almost an hour long, but for Antonia, time passed even slower. Suddenly, she wasn't sure how to act around Sánchez, and she didn't like that feeling.

"Can I ask you something?" she blurted out.

Sánchez frowned, but before she could answer, they were ushered inside a room where Mickey was waiting for them.

"Go on."

Antonia moved closer to the character and stood next to it as Sánchez took her picture. Her cheeks hurt from how wide she was smiling, and across from her, Sánchez smiled back.

"Here you go," Sánchez said, handing the phone to Antonia. "What do you want to do next?" she asked as they walked out.

"A roller coaster! The biggest one they have," Antonia replied. "Oh, and the haunted house!"

Sánchez nodded and took Antonia's hand again. As she was being led through the masses of people walking around, Antonia tried to ignore the way her heart rate increased at the touch.

Camila never expected to use the word "endearing" to refer to Antonia, but she couldn't think of any other way to describe her in that moment. Antonia looked like a small kid as she held a giant ice cream cone in one hand and moved her head from side to side anytime something caught her eyes. She spun the cone around, trying to catch the loose drops of melted vanilla goodness that threatened to slide down her arm. Despite her attention being on the ice cream, she never loosened the hold she had on Camila with her other hand. Camila used the connection to pull Antonia around, navigating the park to take her to yet another attraction. Once in a while she glanced over her shoulder, only to find Antonia tilting her head to lick the underside of the cone. One of those times she stared for a second too long. When their eyes met, Antonia gave her the biggest, toothiest grin she'd ever seen on her. It was too damn cute.

Camila smiled back without meaning to, like the obvious happiness radiating from Antonia had taken over her body and made her forget about anything else on her mind. She snapped her head back to look in front of her as soon as she realized her eyes had lingered for too long on Antonia's lips.

Not looking at Antonia helped calm her racing heart to a degree, but the skin of her fingers still tingled in every place that remained in contact with her. Their day together was feeling more and more like a date as time went on. And what was worse, Camila wished it was one.

Neither of them had mentioned what had happened at the club the night before, but Camila couldn't stop thinking about it. She wasn't sure if she was glad or upset that Antonia was an expert at ignoring the elephant in the room. An expert at pretending nothing had happened. She didn't want to talk about it or have to give an explanation, but she also didn't want to feel like Antonia didn't care.

She wanted to believe that Antonia's feelings for her went beyond sex. And when Antonia smiled at her or held her hand a little tighter, Camila was almost convinced that she did. But then she remembered how every single time after they'd hooked up, Antonia acted as if it was all the same to her if they slept together or not. She'd offered to be friends but never implied she wanted more than that. Camila was always the one throwing herself at Antonia, and she couldn't help but think that Antonia would take the opportunity when it was offered but wasn't interested in more.

Was Camila even interested in more? She didn't know. Maybe. Being with Antonia was easy most of the time. She'd even stopped finding her infuriating and enjoyed working with her on the field. That wasn't enough of a foundation for a relationship, but it was a start. And if Camila allowed herself to be truthful, she sometimes craved having someone who wanted her. Antonia made her feel that way when they were together, but it also seemed easy for her to stay away when Camila asked her for space.

"I'm sorry for dragging you here."

Camila looked at Antonia. "What?"

"You seem somewhere else. I assume you're bored."

"No, I'm not bored. I'm having a lot of fun. And you didn't drag me here. It was my idea."

"I appreciate it," Antonia replied, her fingers grazing Camila's. "Do you think we have time for another ride before the fireworks show?"

Camila smiled. "I think we do, yeah."

As Antonia took off in the direction of the Seven Dwarfs Mine Train, Camila stood rooted in place, watching her retreating form with a weight on her heart.

Fuck. I'm falling for her.

The sky was dyed with a dark blue tint as they walked toward Cinderella Castle. It was way later than advisable to get a good spot for the show, but Antonia had been so happy, so eager to experience as many rides as she could, that time got away from them. As expected, the area was packed when they tried to get there, but Camila had gone to Disney enough times that she'd learned how to maneuver around the crowds to find a spot with a decent view of the fireworks.

They stood side by side, their necks craned in the castle's direction as the projections danced around the walls, bringing those magical worlds to life in a way that almost made Camila wish she could be part of them. She sneaked a look at Antonia only to find a wide smile on her face, her eyes reflecting the lights in front of them.

Their shoulders rubbed together with each accidental push from the surrounding crowd, but the decision to hold her hand was Camila's and Camila's alone. This time, she couldn't pretend it was out of necessity to help them navigate the park better or to pull Antonia in the direction she needed her to go. It was simply because she wanted to. Because she craved the warmth of Antonia's skin and because she wanted to feel the connection growing in her heart in a tangible way. She wanted to reassure herself that Antonia was really there and wanted to hold her hand just as much as Camila did. The little squeeze Antonia gave her erased all vestiges of doubt swirling in her brain, almost as if Antonia had read her mind and knew when and how to offer a sign.

They remained in that position for the whole show, standing next to each other, staring ahead at the lights, but never letting go. Camila wondered if Antonia's heart was hammering the same way as hers. She wanted to place her free hand over Antonia's chest to find out. Instead, she rubbed the back of Antonia's hand in circles with her thumb and squeezed her hand harder when the fireworks started going off around them.

The lights bursting out over the now dark sky were beautiful, bright, and energetic. Just like Antonia. The blue, red, and white lights cast shadows and highlights over her brown skin and her dark, wide eyes. Her eyes darted around, and her mouth was slightly parted as she followed the show with her gaze. Camila forgot about the fireworks and focused on Antonia. The entire time, Camila stared at the angles of Antonia's jaw and the one curl that always fell over her eyes.

She gripped Antonia's hand harder and yanked on it once, twice, until Antonia turned to look at her. As soon as their eyes met, Camila cupped her face. She didn't move for a long ten seconds, part of her wondering what she was doing. But Antonia didn't move either. She gave her all the time in the world, not fazed at all by her behavior. Her gaze went back over the same features she'd already stared at so much, and when she could only find softness and openness in them, she moved forward an inch—daring to get closer to what she wanted, knowing that this time, if she kissed Antonia, it wouldn't be like any of their other kisses. She wasn't sure if she could go back to a world where their mouths touched only because of nothing more than raw passion.

When they melted into one, everything around Camila faded away. It wasn't the first time their lips had met, but it was the first time they kissed like this—slow and steady, savoring every minute. She held Antonia's face between her hands, as if she was afraid of losing her even before fully having her. Their lips moved in perfect sync, and they kissed and kissed, forgetting about the world. For the first time, Camila let the kiss be the goal itself and not just a stop on the way to something else.

When they pulled apart, Camila watched the fireworks reflecting in Antonia's pupils, and she also saw something else she couldn't figure out.

Camila opened her mouth but closed it again without uttering a word. There was no point in saying anything when there was no clarity in her thoughts. She didn't know what the kiss meant or if it changed anything between them. She only knew she'd wanted to do it, and so she did.

Chapter Fifteen

CAMILA HAD BEEN MISERABLE since Antonia left to join Brazil's national team for a campaign of friendly games. They'd returned to Houston after their day at Magic Kingdom, and one week later Antonia was off to be the superstar of her team while Camila remained alone in their empty apartment.

That wasn't what upset her. Okay, maybe a small part of her was a little bitter about it, since she could barely hold on to her position on the Houston Starlight, much less hope to be called to the national team. But no, that wasn't it. The reason she was so upset was because she'd been more vulnerable than ever, having gone and kissed Antonia under the Magic Kingdom fireworks—a soft, slow kiss that shook Camila to her core. And then Antonia never mentioned it or talked about it.

Her mind had been going a hundred miles a minute since then, replaying that one magical kiss time and time again, while it seemed to be just an ordinary kiss for Antonia.

She didn't expect Antonia to profess her undying love, but it had to be obvious how much that kiss meant to Camila. Right? She couldn't believe it didn't spark even a bit of curiosity in Antonia. Until then, they'd only had casual encounters or drunk kisses. It was eating Camila up to not know if that kiss meant as much to Antonia as it did to her, but of course she couldn't ask her. Kissing her like that had made her vulnerable enough. She wasn't about to go and beg Antonia to open up to her.

She was about to leave for the gym, hoping that maybe several hours of exercise could help her channel her frustrations, when a text from Liz inviting her to brunch changed her plans. She considered saying no, but maybe a distraction would help her stop thinking about Antonia. Plus, she also wanted to make Liz tell her about whatever she had going on with López once and for all.

They met at the cute bakery in Montrose that Liz loved, and it took longer for them to be seated than for Liz to start grilling Camila with questions. That wasn't the plan.

"So, are you going to spill on what you have going on with Antonia?"

"I could ask the same about you and López," Camila replied, trying to deflect.

"Oh, I don't have a problem sharing all the juicy details with you. You're the one who loves to pretend you hate Antonia."

"I do hate her," she said vehemently. Liz raised an eyebrow, and Camila cleared her throat. "Well, I used to hate her. Sometimes I still do, to be honest, but not as often."

Liz chuckled. "That was convincing. I totally believed you."

Camila's first instinct was to dismiss Liz again. But she'd been thinking about her situation with Antonia for days, and maybe getting someone else's perspective would help her deal with it and focus on something else at least.

"Fine. We slept together and then we called it off and then she kissed me and then we had like a pseudo-date and now I don't know what any of it means."

"Okay . . . That's a lot," Liz said, taking a sip of her green juice. "You realize you kind of did all the relationship steps backward, right?"

Camila sighed. "That's the thing. We're not in a relationship." She looked away, an image of Antonia flashing in her mind. "And I don't think she wants to be."

"Have you asked her?" Liz replied as if it was the most logical thing in the world.

Camila's only answer was an exasperated look.

"Fine, you don't want to ask her. Do you want a relationship, though?"

She didn't answer at first, struggling to find the words to explain why she was upset. "No," she finally answered. At Liz's scoff, she rushed to clarify. "I don't want to feel like I'm being played. That's all."

"You two are much more of a mess than I thought."

The protest died on Camila's lips. As much as she wanted to deny it, it was the truth. She didn't know how to act around Antonia and had no clue what the other girl wanted. She wasn't even sure what *she* wanted. The worst part was that while she agonized, overthinking every little interaction, Antonia couldn't care less.

Antonia stared at the gray popcorn ceiling of her New York hotel room. While she waited for her agent to pick her up for lunch, her phone rested next to her on the bed, an inch away from her fingertips. She'd thrown it there after typing and deleting a message to Camila for the hundredth time.

Camila. She rolled the name in her mouth in the emptiness of the room, where only she could hear it, saying it out loud one, two, three times. She liked how it sounded. She tried to remember when exactly the hot but infuriating teammate she'd met months before stopped being Sánchez in her mind and became Camila. She wasn't sure—she only knew there had been a change at some point.

After their day at Magic Kingdom, they'd settled on a nice, calm dynamic in the short time they spent together before Antonia had to travel to join the Brazilian national team for a string of friendly games. She wasn't sure if their new, less aggressive relationship was simply an illusion of time and distance, or if maybe something had finally shifted between them permanently, after so much hot and cold.

There was still tension between them. Long silences that stretched on until one of them awkwardly cleared their throat. Lingering looks she pretended to not notice, and she had a feeling Camila did too. The animosity was gone, and they spent the days before she left without a single fight. But Antonia didn't know how to approach the other girl. She didn't know how to handle the whiplash of going from acting friendly, kissing, barely acknowledging each other, and back to kissing again.

She wasn't sure what to expect. She didn't dare hope for it to mean anything more than Camila's usual back-and-forth of using her when she needed comfort and discarding her as soon as it became too much. Antonia had gotten used to it, but since that night at Disney, she couldn't shake the feeling that their kiss had been different. The way Camila had kept her eyes closed long after their mouths drifted apart. The sharp intake of breath once she finally opened them and they looked at each other with the fireworks still going off around them. The way she didn't let go of her hand—not after the kiss, and not while they walked out of the park. All of it told her that the kiss may have been different from all the other kisses before it.

She thought so but didn't dare ask for confirmation. Any time she'd hinted at wanting to talk about their relationship, Camila freaked out and shut her down, and Antonia didn't want to undo the progress they'd made.

Leaving for New York on her own had been a lucky break. A chance to put some distance between them before she blurted out something inappropriate and sent their relationship back to square one again.

Playing for the Brazilian national team was also a wonderful distraction. She loved any chance she got to represent her country, and spending a few days in a locker room filled with laughter and speaking in Portuguese made her feel at home. With her Brazilian teammates, even if she only saw some of them a handful of times a year, there was a natural camaraderie. There was also less competition. They didn't have to fight for a position. They were in the same boat and had the same goal in mind: to make their country proud.

It was only a string of friendly games, but any time Antonia put on that verde e amarela shirt, she played as if it were the final of the World Cup. Seeing the scattered Brazilian flags all over the stadium filled her with energy and purpose. She loved Houston and the Starlight, but it wasn't the same. For at least a couple of days, she felt closer to Brazil than she had in a long time. The closest she could be for the time being.

Once the friendly tour ended, her agent had insisted on taking Antonia out before she returned to Houston the next day. She'd been in New York with another one of her clients and wanted to take advantage of the fact that they both were there so they could talk business. Antonia could use the distraction from obsessing over every single interaction she'd had with Camila. Plus she hoped her good showings with Brazil and the Houston Starlight meant her agent had a lot of endorsement offers that would earn her enough money to help her brother like she wanted.

A text message pinged on her phone. Antonia's heart clenched, wondering for an instant if it was Camila, but of course it wasn't. It was her agent letting her know she was waiting for her downstairs.

"Hey there, superstar."

Antonia smiled. "Hey, Arantxa. Trying to butter me up with that nickname?"

"You already signed with me, so no need to butter you up," Arantxa replied with a smirk of her own. "I know you don't believe me, but you're more popular than you think. I should know. I have several big brands knocking on my door and a couple of teams that would have you in a heartbeat."

"Maybe." Antonia shrugged. "I'm not anywhere close to the fame of Daniela Martínez or your other clients."

"You will be. Trust me."

She wanted to believe her. Not because fame was important to her, but because it meant being closer to her dream of building a better life for her and her brother.

Arantxa insisted on taking her to the US Open final, and it wasn't as if Antonia had anything else to do. Besides, even though she barely knew anything about tennis, she'd had a small crush on Daniela Martínez

214

once upon a time. It was surreal to think they now shared an agent and she could meet her in person.

As Arantxa drove them to the US Open grounds, Antonia couldn't stop herself from checking her phone for the first time in hours. She opened her text exchange with Camila. The last message in the chat was a picture of them at Disney. She considered sending a text, even if just to say hi, but it seemed silly.

"Is that your girlfriend?" Arantxa asked, looking over her shoulder at the picture.

"No. Just a teammate."

Arantxa raised her eyebrows at her but said nothing else.

"It's complicated," Antonia added, feeling exposed by that simple gesture.

Arantxa sighed loudly. "God, exactly what I needed. Another useless lesbian as a client," she said with a smile. "I have no clue what's going on there, but I'll give you some advice in case it applies to you. The only way to know how someone feels is to ask them and show them you're willing to listen."

"I don't think that applies to my situation, but thanks."

"It applies to most situations. Think about it. But for today, let's just have fun."

Antonia nodded, happy to change topics. In the back of her mind, a nagging feeling persisted. She wondered if maybe it really was as easy as Arantxa made it sound. If maybe she just needed to get Camila to talk to her. Yet from her experience, even if she wanted to give that a try, getting Camila to open up was easier said than done.

The apartment felt empty without Antonia. Camila hated to admit it, even if only to herself. But it was too quiet, it didn't smell of food, and it just felt . . . lifeless. She hit one of the preset buttons on the microwave and watched as her TV dinner spun inside for the entire three and a half minutes it took to heat.

The hot plastic container seared the tips of her fingers. That should have been enough warning for her to wait before trying to eat it, but she wasn't paying attention. She ate a spoonful and burned her tongue, rendering the rest of the meal flavorless. Not that there was much flavor to mourn. It was her worst meal in months, not only because of the taste, but because she missed Antonia's laughter and constant chatter while they ate.

When she turned on the TV to chase away the loneliness, the last thing Camila expected to see was Antonia's face staring back at her. She double-checked why that was happening and was even more surprised to realize that Antonia was at the US Open, looking right at home in the middle of Daniela Martínez's player box. It made no sense. Antonia had never mentioned liking tennis or being friends with a famous tennis player. Against her best judgment, she watched the match, only to catch the sporadic glimpses of Antonia.

With no one around her, Camila could allow herself to stare. Antonia only appeared a handful of times for a few seconds, but Camila couldn't help but notice how beautiful she looked. She was wearing a plain white T-shirt with a leather jacket, sunglasses, and jeans, and she looked like a freaking rock star. The other thing she noticed was the stunning woman sitting next to her. The short hair and bright smile caught Camila's eye right away, but it wasn't until they showed her leaning down to whisper something into Antonia's ear that the small, nagging feeling in Camila's chest started.

Camila tried to push the jealousy down, to smother it by reminding herself that it wasn't like she and Antonia were in a relationship. But her brain and her heart were at odds with each other. No matter how much she repeated to herself that she didn't want Antonia, she did, and it stung to see her so close to another woman, especially a woman as beautiful as the one sitting next to her at the US Open.

Rationally, she knew that the attractive woman was Daniela's agent, according to the commentators, and wasn't involved with Antonia at all, but it was eating at Camila knowing she would have no grounds to be upset even if there was something going on between them. She'd pushed Antonia away so many times, it embarrassed her to even think about asking her for more than she'd already given her. Now she realized she wanted her more than she'd dared to admit to herself; she wanted Antonia to become hers and only hers, but she wasn't sure if she was ready to say that out loud and to her face.

A pang of longing hit her when she heard Daniela Martínez's winning speech. She wanted someone to love her like that. Someone who could see beyond her walls, who held her when she needed it most. She opened her phone and looked at the picture she'd taken with Antonia at Disney. Someone like that was already in her life. She just needed to be brave enough to embrace it, even if it scared her.

Chapter Sixteen

CAMILA'S PHONE WAS BLOWING up when she got out of the shower after practice. She heard the incessant pinging of her text messages as she walked to her locker but disregarded it in favor of getting dressed. The text notifications turned into the loud ring of a call, and she could no longer ignore it.

She frowned at her mom's name lighting up the screen; her mom never called her.

"Hey, what's up?" she said.

"Have you checked your messages? I've been trying to reach you for hours," her mom replied with a hint of desperation in her voice Camila had never heard before.

Usually, she would have fired back at her mom with a snarky remark or tried to end the call as soon as possible, but she could tell that whatever had compelled her mom to call her was a serious matter.

"Sorry, I was at practice. I just got out," she mumbled.

"Something happened with your dad. I'm not exactly sure what's happening, but he got arrested this morning."

"What?" Camila's head started spinning. She'd heard what her mom said, but she couldn't make any sense of it. Why on earth would her dad get arrested? "I don't understand."

"I have a meeting with his lawyers later, but it's something about corruption and money laundering. A lot of important FIFA executives seem to be involved, but I don't know all the details. I just wanted you to know before it appears all over the news."

Camila collapsed on the bench, still wrapped in a towel. She tried to process what her mother had told her, but it all seemed so far-fetched and improbable. Her dad, arrested? It couldn't be possible. She opened her phone and did a Google search, only to find a myriad of headlines confirming her mom's words.

Twenty FIFA Executives Arrested for Fraud

Switzerland and US Authorities Dismantle Soccer Corruption Network

Historic Uruguayan Player Ricardo Sánchez Accused of Money Laundering

Her finger hovered over the last headline, afraid of clicking it and opening the article. Afraid of what she would find out about her father if she did. But not knowing was worse.

The more she read, the more horrified she became. According to the articles, her dad had taken part in paying and receiving bribes for getting certain players he'd coached over the past decade onto the national teams of Mexico and Uruguay, with the goal of raising their profile so they could be sold to international teams for more money. He'd also received a bribe for his vote to pick the upcoming World Cup host.

Camila felt like throwing up. She had her issues with her dad, but no matter what, she'd always admired him. She'd always been proud of him. Most of her issues came from feeling like she wasn't good enough to follow in his footsteps. She couldn't believe he was part of something like this. That the man she'd known all her life and admired so much was a criminal. A fraud.

Out of the corner of her eye, she noticed someone checking their phone and then looking at her. She wondered if they were reading the same article she was. If so, soon everyone would know she was the daughter of a corrupt man. If convincing people she'd earned her place on the team based on her own merits had been hard before, she didn't want to imagine what people would think now that her dad had confirmed he wasn't above using his influence for his own benefit.

She got dressed as fast as possible and left without a word to anyone. She didn't want to wait around to see if they'd found out about what happened and then have to avoid their questions.

Sitting in her car in the parking lot, she wondered where to go. Returning to her empty apartment was the last thing she felt like doing. What she wanted was to bury herself in someone's arms and have them whisper comforting words in her ear. No, not just somebody. She wanted someone specifically.

Camila put the car in drive and, without realizing, she took the highway to Galveston. There was nothing for her there either, but it would help her pass the time.

When she got there, she found herself on the same beach where, months before, she'd spent the afternoon with Antonia. She chuckled. Of course she'd been thinking about her. The memory of their day playing soccer and running around the beach brought a smile to her face for an instant.

She walked with her shoes in her hand and then sat on the wet sand, counting the waves as they crashed along the beach. She thought of her dad as she stared at the horizon. She remembered how he'd bought her a soccer ball as soon as she could walk. How, no matter how busy he was, he always played with her as a kid, teaching her the best way to hit the ball and letting her wear his jerseys. One of her favorite memories was of running onto the field after her dad won a championship and him raising her on his shoulders and letting her carry the cup.

Since that day, Camila had become obsessed with one day winning a cup of her own, so her dad could be as proud of her as she was of him. She never imagined that all her admiration for her father would turn into disappointment.

She sat there until the sun disappeared and the wind picked up, blowing away the last remains of her tears. She felt empty, tired. But she couldn't stay at the beach forever. Eventually, she got in her car and drove back to the city.

As soon as she opened the apartment door, the weight of the day crashed into her, making her want to crawl into bed. She was almost there when she noticed the light coming out of Antonia's room.

She was back.

Her feet took her to Antonia's door before she had time to process what she was doing. She cracked the door open to find Antonia unpacking her things.

"Hey," Antonia said with a soft smile.

Camila burst into tears.

That wasn't the reaction Antonia was expecting when she greeted Camila. She'd been looking forward to seeing her, talking herself into trying once again to have an honest conversation with her about her feelings. But all of that was forgotten the minute she saw her tear-stained face.

Antonia felt the urge to take Camila into her arms and protect her from whatever was hurting her. She took a step forward, and not one second after opening her arms as an invitation, Camila buried her head in Antonia's chest and clung to her, sobs wracking her body.

"It's okay. I'm here," Antonia said.

She didn't know what was causing Camila's turmoil. She couldn't offer reassurances when she didn't even know what had the other girl in that state. But she meant what she'd said. No matter what it was, she would be there for her.

"My dad . . . He . . . I c-can't believe it."

"Is he okay? What happened?"

"He's fine. But he's not who I thought he was," Camila said through sniffles. He's a liar. He's . . . I don't even kn-know who he is anymore."

224

The only response Antonia could muster was to hug Camila tighter. She didn't know what else to do or say. When Camila spoke again, her voice was lower. Almost a whisper.

"And I d-don't know who I am anymore if I c-can't be proud of being his daughter," Camila added between sobs.

"You're so much more than just his daughter."

Camila scoffed, and her crying slowed down. "I doubt anyone sees it that way. It sucked to be Camila Sánchez, the daughter of Uruguayan soccer legend Ricardo Sánchez, and have everyone thinking the only reason a team would want me was because of him. But now I'm the daughter of Ricardo Sánchez, a corrupt soccer coach who probably paid to have his daughter on a professional team. That's even worse."

"Fuck what people say or think." Antonia grabbed Camila's face and made her look at her. "You know who you are and how much you've worked to get where you are. Don't let anyone put you down."

Camila moved away and sat on the bed. Antonia followed her, itching to hold her in her arms again, to wrap her in them and pretend nothing could hurt her as long as she held her.

"I wish I could ignore what other people think about me, but I can't. And I know nobody sees me as anything but his daughter," Camila said, looking at the floor.

Antonia used the tip of her finger to raise Camila's head. "I do," she said, looking into her eyes. "I know you're so much more than that."

There were still streaks of tears running down Camila's face, but the sobs stopped. Antonia moved her finger from Camila's chin to her cheeks, wiping away the tears. She knew she couldn't erase the sadness or the pain, but she hoped the gesture would at least ease them a little. Her finger lingered next to Camila's lips, hesitating at the corner of her mouth.

She wanted to trace the pink lips with her finger, or better yet, replace it with her own lips and put into a kiss all the care she had for Camila. She dismissed the idea as soon as it popped up and moved the finger away, until Camila caught her hand and raised the fingers to her lips and planted a string of small kisses on the tips of them. Camila moved closer, lips hovering over Antonia's for one excruciating second, before meeting in a slow kiss. Neither of them tried to escalate, neither of them reached to tear off clothes or pushed a tongue between parted lips. They let their mouths dance together without further expectations.

Antonia opened her eyes as slowly as their lips had moved during the kiss a few instants before. When she did, she found deep hazel eyes opening slowly too and staring back at her. Camila leaned down once again, this time with more force and desperation, using the weight of her body to push Antonia onto the bed.

She struggled to react, confused by the sudden change and aware of how vulnerable Camila was in that moment. She gathered all her strength and pushed Camila away. When she met questioning eyes, she tried to find the words to explain why she couldn't go further.

"I don't want you to regret this tomorrow," Antonia said.

"I won't," Camila pleaded.

"You can't know that yet, and I'd rather not risk it. I'll hold you instead."

Tears started welling in Camila's eyes again. "See, even you don't want me."

Antonia's heart broke at those words, but they also confirmed she was making the right choice. She caressed Camila's face and gave her a kiss, slow enough that she hoped it would show Camila how much she wanted her, but short enough that she couldn't think Antonia didn't mean what she said about choosing not to go further that night.

"You're wrong. I want you so much. That's why I'm stopping."

Antonia wasn't sure if her words would make sense, but Camila nodded and nestled her head in her chest, holding her tight as her breathing slowed down.

Antonia's smell invaded Camila's senses as soon as she opened her eyes in the morning and realized that her nose was buried in Antonia's neck. Her first impulse was to move away, put as much distance as possible between them. The thought of facing Antonia after the way she'd melted down in her arms the night before was too much for her to bear. The problem was that everything about Antonia—the warmth of her body, her smell, her closeness—comforted her, and Camila craved that comfort. She still wanted to hide in Antonia's hair and stay there, away from the rest of the world, for as long as she could.

Those two conflicting feelings wrestled inside of her until the need for comfort won over. It was impossible to humiliate herself more than she already had the night before, so what did it matter if she stayed in bed with Antonia? Camila closed her eyes again and allowed her body to relax in Antonia's embrace. She couldn't stay there forever, but she would enjoy it for as long as she could.

The chiming of her phone kept trying to pull her out of the safe haven of Antonia's arms. Camila imagined it was more messages from her mom that she didn't want to read, so she ignored them the best she could until Antonia woke up.

"Please get that or turn your phone off," Antonia mumbled half-asleep, pulling Camila closer against her chest.

Begrudgingly, Camila extracted herself from Antonia's arms and checked her phone. She found messages not only from her mom but also from several teammates. Coach Medina was apparently also linked to the corruption scandal but not yet arrested, and the team had suspended him from his position pending an investigation.

Another message—this one from Coach Megan—asked her to stop by her office before practice. Camila groaned and threw her now turned-off phone on the bed, anticipating that no matter what she did or wanted, she would be involved in the entire ordeal because of her dad.

"I'll make you breakfast. That will make you feel better," Antonia said, now wide awake and standing next to her. She leaned down almost as if she wanted to kiss Camila, but at the last minute stopped and walked away.

Camila stayed in bed until the smell of pancakes filled the apartment. Her stomach was in knots, and she doubted she could push anything down, but the need to be close to Antonia led her to the kitchen.

Antonia's bright smile greeted her from the other side of the counter. A second later there was a plate full of pancakes with candied strawberries and whipped cream in front of her, as well as a steaming mug of coffee.

"I made your favorites," Antonia said.

A sad smile was all Camila could return. She picked at the food while Antonia moved around in the kitchen. A warm feeling spread in Camila's chest at the way Antonia tried her best to distract her. It felt nice to be taken care of, but a nagging feeling in the back of her mind made her wonder why Antonia was doing it. Not to mention the fact that she'd rejected her advances the night before, and Camila wasn't sure how to feel about that. Being humiliated at the rejection would be her first instinct, but there was something about the way Antonia had pushed her away, about how she'd whispered against her hair that she wanted her and held her close, that had Camila's mind spinning.

She'd been so confused after their kind-of date at Disney, after that slow, languid kiss they'd shared under the fireworks. And right when she'd convinced herself that it meant nothing, Antonia threw her for a loop again with how caring and supportive she was.

Camila's pancakes were pretty much untouched by the time Antonia put a plate with eggs and bacon next to it.

"Please, eat a little. I swear it will help you feel better," Antonia said as she sat next to Camila with her own plate full of pancakes. "Here, you need more whipped cream. That's the problem," she added. Before Camila could react, she drew a smiley face with the whipped cream on top of her pancakes.

Camila couldn't help but smile. "That's what was missing."

For a few long minutes, the only sound in the apartment was the clattering of forks and knives, until Camila couldn't keep the thoughts that were swirling in her mind in check any longer. "What are we?" she blurted.

Antonia stopped her movements midbite, her mouth hanging open while a strawberry slid down her fork. It would have been a comical image for Camila to enjoy if she wasn't so preoccupied with the potential answer.

"What do you mean?" Antonia replied.

"You told me you wanted to be my friend, but then you kissed me back in Orlando. You held me last night but refused to have sex with me because you care too much about me, and now you're making me breakfast," Camila retorted, her voice becoming quieter with each word. "It confuses me. You confuse me."

The fork clinked against the plate when Antonia dropped it. She turned around and cupped Camila's face, making her heart skip a beat.

"I'm your friend," Antonia said. "I've always wanted to be your friend."

Camila's heart dropped in her chest. She scoffed and moved her head away from Antonia's touch, unable to bear seeing the softness in her eyes that was being directed at her. Of course that was all Antonia meant—pity disguised as friendship. A biting remark lingered on the tip of her tongue, ready to push Antonia away, but the other girl beat her to speaking.

"Look at me. Look at me, please."

The way she moved her head around as she tried to find Camila's eyes and the way she kept rubbing her thumb over her cheek made it hard for Camila's anger to take over. Maybe she'd exhausted her energy being mad at her dad and she didn't have enough to resist Antonia.

"I want to be your friend, your support, the person you lean on. I want to be there for you," she said, moving Camila's chin gently so they sat face-to-face. "That doesn't mean I don't want to be more than that too, but those three things are the most important. You confuse me too. Most of the time, you act like you don't want me around. You've rejected me over and over. I don't know what you want, but I'm still here. And I will be here as long as you need me. If we become more than friends, that depends on you."

Camila lowered her gaze, unable to stand looking into Antonia's sincere eyes. She had to admit she was right. She had been the one who had put a stop to any romantic evolution in their relationship. She wished it was as easy as Antonia made it sound, that it was simply a matter of saying, "Yes, I want to give this a try." But the truth of the matter was that even as she asked Antonia for more, now that she offered it to Camila, the fear came back stronger than ever.

Opening the door to something more with Antonia also opened her up to the possibility of being hurt. And in that moment, with everything else going on, she didn't think she could handle any kind of relationship drama. Being friends was easier. Safer.

Except for two minor facts: the way she craved the comfort of Antonia's arms and how her kisses were the one thing that could help her forget the shitshow that was her life.

The idea of saying those thoughts out loud seemed ridiculous, but Antonia's inviting face made it seem a little less so. The other girl had always been honest with her—painfully so. Maybe just telling her what she wanted wouldn't be as bad as she thought.

"Right now, friends sounds like just what I need. Like the safe choice."

Antonia smiled as she ran her thumb up and down Camila's cheek and then nodded. Not one ounce of judgment in her expression.

That made it easier for Camila to finish what she wanted to say.

"But I know it's not all I want. I'm not sure how it happened, but you've taken over my heart, and I need you to kiss me right now."

Antonia didn't need to be told twice. As soon as Camila looked at her with those enormous hazel eyes glistening with unshed tears and asked for a kiss, Antonia leaned over. In that moment, she didn't care about analyzing the fact that, once again, she wasn't sure if they'd ended as friends or more, but it didn't matter. What they had, even if it didn't have a name, was an unbreakable link that brought them together time and again.

They may not have a label, but what was a relationship if not a combination of all the things they were, all the things they'd been? Friends, lovers, rivals. In the end, they both knew they wanted each other, they sought each other, and they always came together as one.

Antonia stroked Camila's cheek and stopped to look into her eyes when a shaky breath left her lips. She drank in every detail of Camila's face and the way she closed her eyes before Antonia even moved. She leaned forward slowly, as slow as possible, letting their breaths mix in anticipation of the taste of soft lips against her own. Her mouth moved with purpose, and she willed it to speak the words she'd already said out loud. Words she wasn't sure Camila believed. *I care about you. I want you. I'm here for you.*

Camila grasped Antonia's wrists, nails digging into her skin as if asking her to never let her go. To never stop kissing her. Antonia didn't want to stop. Every touch made her crave Camila more, but she knew she needed to end the kiss. It was meant to be a short, comforting gesture, but the risk of it becoming more than that grew with every second their lips remained connected.

She moved away, only an inch, enough for there to be space between them but close enough that she still could gaze into Camila's eyes and try to convey with one look everything she felt. The swirl of emotions in those pupils staring right at her almost broke her and made her want to lean in again to erase the pain, but she didn't. She couldn't.

One kiss—that was all Camila had asked for, and all Antonia should give her. Kissing her again would blur the line between comfort and something more. The last thing Antonia wanted was to bring more confusion and worries into Camila's life.

"I'm here for you," she said, moving away from her.

"Thank you," Camila answered with a small smile that didn't reach her eyes. "Thank you for being my friend, even when I told you I didn't want you to be."

"Of course. I'll always be here for you, I promise."

And Antonia meant it. She cared about Camila, and she wanted to erase that haunted look from her face. She wanted to push the weight off her shoulders and help her breathe again.

Chapter Seventeen

THE IDEA OF BEING kicked off the team never occurred to Camila. Not the day before when she found out about her father's problems, nor that morning when the assistant coach asked to speak to her. It never crossed her mind that the scandal would affect her, besides the shame it brought her to find out her dad was a corrupt man. It didn't occur to her, but it should have.

Of course the logical conclusion most people would reach after finding out that her father had deals with high FIFA officials, teams, and sponsors to arrange transfers and earn money by inflating a player's value was that he had used those same tactics and connections to advance his own daughter's career. Camila wanted to scream that it wasn't true. That she'd earned her place on the team by her own merit, but she couldn't because she wasn't sure it was true. She'd always thought her dad used his friendships a little too much in her favor—she just never thought there was an entire corrupt network involved in it. And to be honest, she didn't put it past him to do the same for her because he thought she couldn't make it on her own.

That's why the news about her suspension, pending an internal investigation, left her numb more than anything else. She hated it, but she understood why the team had done it. They didn't have any other option if they wanted to keep their image clean.

"I hope you understand it's nothing personal," Coach Megan told her. "You're a great player, and I'm sure you will be back playing with the team in no time. This is just procedure."

Camila nodded. It wasn't like she could do anything to change the situation.

"You'll be allowed to train with the rest of the team, but you won't be eligible to play in any of the upcoming matches until the investigation is closed. That means you'll likely miss most of the playoff games that are coming up."

"I understand," Camila answered, but her voice sounded empty to her own ears.

Antonia was waiting for her outside the office. She'd offered to go early with her when she told her Coach

Megan needed to meet with her. Seeing Antonia, all soft smiles and gentle eyes, was almost too much for her and almost made her break down. But she forced herself to contain the tears that were threatening to escape.

Camila's acting skills weren't as good as she had hoped because in less than a second, Antonia was by her side. One hand squeezed her shoulder. "Hey, what happened?"

"I'm suspended." Camila took a deep breath. "The team is opening an investigation to make sure my dad and Coach Medina didn't have any kind of illegal arrangement to get me on the team. I won't be playing for a few weeks, or as long as their investigation takes."

"That's bullshit!" Antonia said. "Everyone with eyes can see you're an amazing player. And this scandal is about male players, not women's football. It's ridiculous that they're punishing you for his sins."

Antonia's words brought Camila some comfort. At least there was someone out there who believed her.

"I get why they're doing it. It's a PR thing more than anything," Camila said. "They have to show they're doing something because the press is going to be asking those same questions. It sucks, but I get it."

"Can you at least train with us?"

"Yeah, I can train."

"What do you say to a one-on-one match before everybody else gets here?" Antonia said with a huge grin on her face and almost bouncing in place with excitement.

For the first time in the past several hours, Camila felt a genuine smile on her lips. "That sounds great, actually."

They walked in silence to the field. Antonia strode ahead with her usual energetic pace while Camila watched her from behind, comforted by her enthusiasm instead of annoyed by it like she used to be. Once on the field, Antonia grabbed a soccer ball and ran to the center of the grass.

"Come on! Get out here so I can kick your ass!" Antonia exclaimed, bouncing the ball on her knee.

Camila watched her from afar, not quickening her pace to reach her. As she walked and looked at Antonia's smiling face, a sense of calm washed over her. Everything faded away from her mind. She didn't think about her dad or her worries. Instead she focused on Antonia, the way she moved, and the happiness that radiated from her as she goofed around with the ball on her feet. Camila tried to remember the last time she'd been that happy while playing and she couldn't. For a while now, soccer had been a chore, an obligation, instead of something she loved to do like when she was a kid. But Antonia made it seem fun again, at least while it was only the two of them.

She jogged the last couple of feet and receive a pass from Antonia as soon as she was close enough.

Camila dribbled on her own at first, bouncing the ball from one foot to the other and stepping on it for a 180-degree spin before passing it back. "You're not the only one who can show off."

"Oh yeah? Let's see if you can match this," Antonia replied. She started with a rainbow kick by launching the ball over her head with the back of her heel. Then she performed knee and foot dribbles. Finally, she ended with catching the ball between her shoulder blades, turning around, and catching it again with the tip of her foot and pushing it in Camila's direction.

Camila smirked but didn't back down from the challenge, replicating each one of Antonia's moves and juggling the ball with her head five times before returning the ball to her.

This time Antonia ran around her, doing dribbles and taunting Camila to goad her into taking the ball from her. Camila rolled her eyes but ran after her, trying to kick away the ball. When Antonia pulled the famous 360-degree Zidane move, she couldn't take it anymore.

"You're just showing off now," Camila said, grabbing Antonia's shirt at her waist and pulling her toward her.

The forward momentum made Antonia stumble and crash into Camila, and the ball rolled away. Neither moved to put distance between them. They stood close together, bodies touching almost everywhere and breaths mixing because of the proximity. Camila couldn't take the way Antonia's eyes pierced hers. Those brown eyes seemed to look into her soul, making her feel exposed. Moving her gaze down proved to be an awful choice since her eyes landed on partially open red lips instead, and the sight overwhelmed her with a need to lean forward and capture them in a searing kiss.

Camila still didn't understand how Antonia had the power to make her forget all her problems. In that moment, her thoughts were only about how much she wanted Antonia and how she wanted to lose herself in her arms. She noticed Antonia staring back at her lips and leaning in. Camila closed her eyes, awaiting the touch of the soft lips she was already so familiar with, but it never arrived. Instead, she felt Antonia's forehead rest against her own for a second before the other girl stepped away.

Antonia closed her eyes and inhaled deeply, filling her nose with the smell of Camila's shampoo. It was becoming harder and harder to not want to kiss and hold her all the time, especially when she let her walls down and that beautiful laugh broke free. What Antonia wanted was to close the gap between them and take Camila's lower lip between her own. They stood close together until Antonia saw several of their teammates walking toward them out of the corner of her eye and stepped away.

Young was the first to reach them and immediately hugged Camila.

"How are you holding up?" she asked, her usual warmth shining through.

"I'm suspended until further notice." Camila shrugged, trying to appear unaffected, but the way she avoided meeting everyone else's eyes told Antonia another story.

Young squeezed Camila's shoulder. "That sucks. I'm sorry."

Camila gave a small, sad smile. "It is what it is. You guys have to win the next couple of matches without me saving your asses," she added with a smirk.

Despite the calm exterior Camila was trying to project, Antonia could tell it was all a front. Her shoulders slumped, and she looked down as she spoke. Antonia wished there was something she could do to help, but she knew they could only wait and hope for the best. She squeezed Camila's hand, hoping the gesture was enough to show her that she intended to have her back. Camila squeezed back, and Antonia could only interpret that as her way of saying she appreciated her support.

"Okay, everyone," Coach Megan called, interrupting their impromptu meeting. "Before we start, I guess everybody knows what's been going on and why Coach Medina won't be with us for the time being. I know this is a complicated situation, but all we can do is let things run their course and focus on training and winning our upcoming matches. Can I count on all of you to do that?"

"Yes, Coach," a chorus of voices answered.

She nodded. "Good. Sánchez, I'll have you training separate from the rest of the team for now, so wait for me here while I set everyone else up," the coach said with what looked like genuine regret. "The rest of you, move it!"

Antonia stood back while their teammates followed the coach.

"Go," Camila said. "I'm okay. Really."

Antonia nodded, but letting go of her hand turned out to be harder than she expected. "Do you want to have dinner with me tonight? I'll cook."

She said it to give Camila something to look forward to later, and mostly because she wanted to bring an ounce of happiness back to those hazel eyes she'd gotten used to seeing full of fire. She wanted to do something nice for Camila. Help her forget the situation she was in.

"Carvalho, we're waiting for you," Coach Megan called from the other side of the pitch.

She poked Camila's nose with her finger. "I'll make your favorite," she said, jogging away.

Training wasn't as awful as Camila expected. It sucked to be separated from the team, but everyone had been supportive, which was an immense relief since her worst fear was being rejected by her own teammates. If they were on her side, she could bear anything.

Leaving practice with Antonia like she'd done countless times before felt so ordinary that she could almost forget the situation with her dad. She'd just started driving when Antonia told her they needed to stop at the grocery store.

"Why?" Camila asked.

"I can't cook your favorite dish if we don't have any food."

"Do you even know what my favorite dish is?"

"Nope, but I'm hoping you'll tell me," Antonia answered with that infuriatingly cute smirk she hated.

But who was she trying to fool anymore? She loved that arrogant expression now.

She glanced at Antonia out of the corner of her eye. There were so many things she wanted to ask. Or maybe just one: Why? Why was she so nice, so attractive, and so damn considerate that Camila couldn't resist her even if she wanted to? She would know—she'd already tried and failed.

"Chicken wings and a beer sound heavenly right now," she said instead. Letting Antonia in wasn't so bad.

Antonia beamed back at her. "Well, it's your lucky day because I make the most amazing crispy chicken wings."

"You know we can just stop on the way home and get takeout, right?"

"Sure, but it wouldn't be the same. They wouldn't have my secret touch."

Camila couldn't help but laugh at Antonia's antics. "Oh? Is that so? What's the secret touch?"

Antonia looked at her for a long time without answering, and for a second Camila thought she was going to say the secret ingredient was love.

"Well, it wouldn't be a secret if I told you," Antonia said instead.

Camila pushed down the disappointment at the answer. Things had changed between them. That much was true. She had allowed herself to lower her walls around Antonia, but thinking of calling what had been growing between them "love" was a step too far.

Yet her heart dropped in disappointment anyway.

Back at the apartment, Antonia went right to work on the food while Camila watched from the couch. Next to her, her phone lit up with messages. Some were from her mother, some were from friends, and some were even from news outlets trying to get a quote. She ignored all of them. Eventually, she would have to confront what was happening, talk to her parents, and get a lawyer, but she was going to put that off as long as possible. Maybe if she didn't think about it, it would go away.

The doorbell rang, and Camila jumped. Before she could react, Antonia answered her unasked question.

"Can you get that? It must be López and Young. I invited them over."

Camila rose from the couch, not sure if she wanted the extra company around. Before opening the door, she plastered a big, fake smile on her face, the same one she reserved for the high society events her mother forced her to go to.

"Hey," she said, moving away to let López and Liz in.

"Hey, girl! We got you some of that craft beer you like," Liz said. She handed her a six-pack of what was indeed one of her favorite beers.

"Thank you," she answered, and the huge fake grin on her face turned into a small, but real, smile. She knew it was their way of showing they cared.

"We also got a bunch of board games. It's gonna be a wild night," López added, waggling her eyebrows.

Camila let out a small laugh. "Sounds amazing."

"Food is almost ready," Antonia told them from the kitchen.

While Liz and López set up a Jenga tower on the living room table, Camila walked into the kitchen. Antonia was serving the wings on a platter, and Camila grabbed her hand.

"Thank you," she said softly.

"You have nothing to thank me for."

Camila squeezed Antonia's hand. "Thank you anyway."

She wanted to do so much more. The urge to lean down and kiss Antonia just to thank her was almost impossible to control, but she did. It was not the time to do it, but Camila wondered why she was trying so hard to stop herself from having what she wanted.

As the night advanced, the light returned to Camila's eyes. Antonia watched her smile become bigger and brighter, and the tension left her shoulders. Camila laughed when López threw the Jenga tower to the floor in only the second round of playing, and she snorted in the most adorable way when López claimed they'd rigged it somehow to make her lose.

They switched to Clue after that to avoid López's wrath. Not that it stopped her from claiming they were cheating every time she lost, but at least there were no falling objects around to make it worse.

"It was Colonel Mustard in the billiard room with a candlestick," Camila said, checking the envelope with the cards. "And . . . I win!" she added triumphantly.

"No way you won again. You're cheating!" López exclaimed.

"You need to learn to lose, López," Antonia replied, flinging a piece of popcorn in her direction.

"You two are sitting way too close together. She probably saw all of your cards. It's the only explanation."

"Babe," Liz whispered.

López ignored the soft warning and doubled down.

Camila rolled her eyes. "Liz is sitting on your lap. There's no way she didn't see your cards."

Antonia wanted to laugh at López's attitude. She was such a sore loser. Usually, she didn't mind it since they were on the same team and it only meant that she gave it her all on the pitch. But it was getting ridiculous during a game night that was supposed to help Camila relax, not end up with all of them fighting over freaking Clue. Looking to her side, she noticed Camila shaking her head and smiling at López's antics. At least their friend's presence was doing its work in that regard.

"Well, we're dating," López said. "It's like an unspoken rule that couples play together. If you're going to keep pretending you don't have the hots for each other, then you can't use that advantage designed only for couples."

Before Antonia could react, Liz did her the favor of punching López's leg to make her shut up. Out of the corner of her eye, she glanced at Camila, hoping López's indiscretion hadn't affected her mood after she'd worked so hard to distract her, but Camila laughed and surprised Antonia by squeezing her hand.

"You're just jealous because even teaming up, you couldn't beat me," Camila shot back.

Antonia was glad López didn't ruin the mood, but she still shot her a death glare while Camila wasn't looking.

One hour later, after a ruthless game of charades that López and Liz also lost, they said their goodbyes. Antonia and Camila picked up the dishes in silence, content to spend time together without talking about heavy topics—just being. A yawn betrayed Camila, letting Antonia know how tired she was after a long two days of emotional turmoil.

"Go to bed. I'll take care of cleaning up," Antonia said as they finished putting the dishes in the sink.

"You've already done too much for me. The least I can do is help with the dishes."

Antonia put her hand on top of Camila's, stopping her from grabbing a plate. "Nonsense. Let me take care of you, at least for today."

Camila ducked her head with a slight blush to her cheeks in what was the most adorable thing Antonia had ever seen.

"Okay, I'm going to get ready for bed, then," Camila replied.

As Antonia watched her walk away, a warm feeling spread in her chest. The urge to protect Camila, to make her smile, was growing by the second.

She'd just finished cleaning the kitchen when Camila returned wearing the cutest kitten pajamas. She stood at the edge of the room, fidgeting with the bottom of her shorts.

"Hey," Antonia said. "What's up?"

It was impossible for her to hear Camila's answer, which was barely above a whisper. Antonia walked toward her, stopping a foot away, and lifted her chin.

"What was that?"

"Would you hold me tonight?" Camila said, eyes fixed on the ground. "I don't want to sleep alone."

Antonia smiled. "Of course. I'll always hold you if you'll have me."

Chapter Eighteen

I⟶ BECAME IMPOSSIBLE TO avoid her father anymore once he was out of custody, and even more so after he showed up in Houston. He and her mom appeared at the stadium one day, and Camila had no option but to go with them. She didn't know if she should feel thankful or annoyed that they chose to take her to a fancy restaurant for a conversation, as if her dad being a corrupt official was something they could talk through over brunch. Apparently, for them it was.

Camila could barely push any food down while her parents seemed to not realize how conflicted she was. Or they were doing a great job pretending not to notice. Her dad kept talking about the Houston Starlight being a strong candidate for the championship, as if Camila hadn't just told them that she'd been suspended from the team. As if he didn't know they had suspended his own friend from his post as coach.

She threw her fork on her plate. "Are you going to spend all day acting as though nothing has happened?"

"Do you always have to ruin everything?" her mom snapped, but she fell silent as soon as her dad raised a hand to stop her.

"I wasn't aware you wanted to talk about the topic," her dad said. "I don't think it's anything you should worry about, but if you want to talk about it, go ahead."

Camila shook her head. "Are you hearing yourself? I found out on the news that my dad was part of a global corruption network, and I got suspended from my team because of it. Even if I get my spot back, everyone will always think the only reason I'm there is because you paid for it. Don't you care about that at all?" She struggled to keep her voice down.

"Cariño, there's nothing to worry about. This whole thing will be over soon, and I'll be back to coaching as usual. I may have to pay a fine, but that's it. The press is making things out to be worse than they are. I don't see what's wrong with a group of friends helping each other out."

Camila scoffed, but that didn't stop her dad from continuing.

"As for your suspension, I'll sort that out. Don't worry. You're my daughter. You have my talent running through your veins, and you shouldn't care what other people say."

She couldn't believe how unapologetic he was. Well, actually, she could. It was not like he'd ever been anything less than extremely self-assured, bordering on arrogant. She knew that trying to make him see reason was a waste of time, but there was one thing she wouldn't allow—for him to mess with her career even more.

"What do you mean, you'll fix it? The last thing I need is you trying to intervene. Stay out of it."

She was going to leave it at that, but the urge to confirm what she'd always suspected was too strong. Part of her didn't want to hear it, but she knew the nagging feeling in the back of her mind would be there forever until she asked. She was afraid of the answer, but maybe knowing for sure would help her move on.

"Did you ever use your influence to get me on a team?" she asked.

"What's the point of having friends in the sport if I won't use them? Of course I did. I reached out to people to give them a little nudge all the time."

He said it as if it was nothing. As if she should be happy about it, instead of demoralized over confirming her suspicious. She'd claimed over and over that it was only her talent doing the talking, but in reality, it'd always been him pulling the strings.

Camila threw her hands up. "The worst part is that you don't even realize why what you're saying is a problem."

"Don't be such a drama queen," her mom interjected. "Didn't you always say you wanted to be a professional player? We were only helping you. You should be more grateful."

Camila pushed her half-eaten eggs away. "I'm leaving. I've lost my appetite, and I can't stand looking at you right now." She got up with more force than intended, making her chair screech against the hardwood floor. "I don't know if I'll ever be able to look at you again. Stay out of my career. I don't want your help. I want nothing to do with you."

She left the table before they could say anything. She threw one last look in their direction when she reached the door. Her dad was standing, mouth agape as he looked at her, but he made no effort to stop her.

Her chest ached. It hurt to leave. It hurt to admit to herself that she needed to walk away from them. From their influence and their expectations. To be able to do what she'd always wanted to do: stand on her own.

The sound of the running shower greeted Camila when she returned to the apartment, bringing her an instant sense of relief because it meant Antonia was home. While waiting for her to finish her shower, she prepared some snacks and picked a movie to watch on Netflix. Imagining an afternoon curled up against Antonia's side as they watched one of her favorite action movies perked up her mood after the disaster of a brunch with her parents.

She'd finished melting cheese in the microwave for some nachos when Antonia's voice carried from her room all the way to the kitchen. Almost without realizing, hypnotized by Antonia's apparent happiness, she walked closer to the bedroom door.

"That sounds great, yeah. You know I'm all for a European team, and Lyon's offer sounds good," she heard Antonia say. "I trust you. Send the terms over, and I'll look over them and let you know."

Camila tried to make sense of what she was hearing. Was Antonia considering joining another team? She didn't have time to dwell on it because the door opened in her face.

"Oh! Hey! Do you want nachos?" Camila asked in a poor attempt to hide her eavesdropping.

"Sure."

Antonia seemed to not have noticed Camila's indiscretion, or she opted for ignoring it. They sat on the couch and started the movie, but instead of relaxing, Camila found herself on edge. The few words she'd heard ran through her head. Antonia opened an email on her phone, but no matter how much Camila tried to see what it said, she couldn't. The uncertainty was too much for her to bear. She needed to know if Antonia was planning on leaving.

"What's that?" Camila asked as casually as she could.

"Oh, it's a contract my agent sent over. I have a couple of teams offering me options."

Camila didn't understand how Antonia could say it so casually while her own heart was shattering into a thousand pieces. She tried to push down the emotions and hide how much it bothered her. "I didn't know you weren't happy in Houston."

Antonia looked at her with inquisitive eyes. "I love Houston, but European teams pay better, and I have to think about what's better for me and my brother."

Camila pushed herself away from Antonia's arms, moving all the way to the other side of the couch. "So you're leaving."

Antonia narrowed her eyes at Camila. "I haven't decided yet. I'm still looking at the options, but maybe." She shrugged. "I don't know."

Camila looked away and stood up.

"Why are you upset?" Antonia asked.

"I'm not upset," Camila rushed to say. But she was halfway to her room, her shoulders were tense, and her voice came out sharp when she answered, making it obvious her words weren't true.

"I haven't decided yet. But if I leave, would you care?" Antonia said, walking into her space.

"Are you serious right now? Of course I'd care if you leave." Camila wanted her tone to be angry, but it come out softer. Broken.

Maybe it was unfair to expect so much from Antonia. She'd been her refuge amid the storm, but Camila hadn't offered anything back. She'd taken Antonia's care and gotten used to it, and she'd assumed it would always be there without stopping to wonder what Antonia may need.

Antonia sighed and grabbed her face. "You say it as if it's the most obvious thing in the world, but it isn't. Half the time, I don't know if you want to kiss me or punch me in the face."

"Sometimes it's both," Camila said with a hint of teasing in her voice.

Antonia smiled back. "That checks out," she said, running her thumb over Camila's mouth. "I think I've made it pretty clear that I like you. But in case it wasn't clear, I do. All this time you've made it a point to push me away, but then you turn around and do something like this that tells me the opposite." She sighed. "I guess what I'm trying to say is that I need you to be clear with me. I need you to say it out loud. The last thing I want is to hurt you, but it's hard for me when I don't even know what to expect or where we stand."

Camila felt overwhelmed by the urge to run away, lock herself in her room, and ignore Antonia until she forgot about their conversation, but the touch of Antonia's fingers kept her grounded in place. She'd already lost everything else that mattered in her life. She didn't want to lose Antonia too. And at least in this case, she had the power to change things.

She took a deep breath, still not sure what she was going to say but knowing she needed to say something.

"I hate you so much," she started, and Antonia smiled because she had to know how fake that statement was no matter how hard Camila tried to cling to it. "What I hate the most is how much I want you in my life. How much better you make my days. How you are the only person who makes me smile." Camila reached for Antonia's hand, which still lingered over her lips, and pecked the tip of her finger. "I like you. A lot. And the more time we spend together, the more I like you, and that's pretty fucking scary."

"Feelings shouldn't be scary. They're what make us truly alive. Just let yourself feel them."

"What if I get hurt?" she whispered.

As Camila talked, Antonia had been moving closer to her, to the point her breath tickled Camila's lips. "Sometimes the pain is worth it," Antonia said, and she closed the distance between them.

Camila got lost in the soft, slow kiss, which warmed her from head to toe. Antonia took Camila's lower lip between her own and sucked on it. Camila's entire body felt like it was on fire, but most of all, her heart fluttered. When the kiss ended, their lips remained connected but immobile as they breathed in each other's air.

"I won't lie to you. I'm probably going to leave," Antonia said without breaking their embrace or moving away, "but before I go, would you give me a chance to show you how good we can be together?"

"What's the point if you're leaving?"

"What's the point of life if not to live it? Why stop ourselves from being happy now just because we don't know what the future will bring? I may stay or maybe not, but we will always have whatever we build with the time we have."

Camila hadn't opened her eyes since their lips first touched, afraid that when she did, the spell would break and the magic would end. Yet as Antonia's words danced in her head, she felt the urge to look into her bright brown eyes. She'd denied herself the chance to be with Antonia—really be with her—all year, for stupid reasons. Even in that moment, there was a list in her mind of all the justifications she could use to spare her heart. But Antonia's eyes were all softness and warmth, and Camila wondered why she was denying herself the chance to be happy, even if it was short-lived.

When Antonia's thumb grazed her lip softly, all excuses went out the window. She had already wasted too much time. She didn't want to waste her last chance.

Instead of speaking, she leaned forward and captured Antonia's lips in a searing kiss. Her hands started roaming, tugging at Antonia's shirt and struggling to touch any part of skin she could reach. Her fingers were making their way to Antonia's breasts under her white tank top when a firm push on her shoulders stopped Camila in her tracks.

"Wait," Antonia mumbled against her lips. "What does this mean?" She stepped away.

Camila grabbed her waist and pulled her closer again. "It means I like you. More than like you. And I want you for as long as I can have you, no matter how long or how short that is."

Antonia smiled and met her halfway in another passionate kiss, her hands grabbing Camila's waist and lifting her up in one swift movement. The only thing

Camila could do was wrap her legs around Antonia in response.

Under other circumstances, Camila would have felt embarrassed about the sound that came out of her mouth, a mix between a whimper and a moan, when her center pressed against Antonia's stomach, but she no longer cared. They stumbled around the apartment, kissing and nipping at each other's necks, until they made it to Antonia's room and the other girl lowered both of them onto the mattress.

Antonia paused for a second, pressing her forehead against Camila's and staring at her for what seemed like an eternity. Camila felt as if Antonia was looking into her soul, but for the first time, she didn't get scared.

She realized that if she took the time to search Antonia's eyes, she could see her soul too.

Every kiss was a new discovery for Antonia because this time she could take her time and put all her feelings into every kiss without fear of it being too much. She didn't have to be afraid of Camila realizing how much she felt for her.

For a long time, Antonia only kissed her, nothing more. She was in no rush to do anything else because she was no longer afraid it would be the only chance she'd get. She took Camila's lips between her own and sucked on them, then moved away and nipped at her neck and shoulders before moving up to connect their lips again.

She let her tongue wander and dance with Camila's in a give-and-take, push-and-pull that alternated between slow and measured, intense and passionate. No matter how she changed the pace, Camila met her halfway every single time.

She'd have spent the night just kissing Camila, savoring her taste and letting her hands roam lightly over her sides, if it wasn't for the way Camila grabbed the back of her neck to bring them closer together and pushed her tongue inside her mouth with force. When they parted their mouths, they stayed close to each other, breathing heavily.

"Please. I need you," Camila breathed.

A wave of desire unraveled inside Antonia. She answered by kissing Camila again, sucking her tongue as soon as she felt it making its way into her mouth. She moved away to plant kisses all over her neck, then down her chest and stomach, until she reached the bottom of her shirt and pushed it up to introduce Camila's naked skin to the warmth of her mouth. She licked along the edge of Camila's waistband, grinning when the other girl let out a moan and her hips bucked against her mouth.

The panting breaths told Antonia everything she needed to know, but it didn't hurt that Camila decided to not be shy about what she wanted either.

"You're set on torturing me tonight, aren't you?" Camila said in a low voice.

"It seemed to me like you were enjoying yourself."

"Oh, I'm enjoying it. Doesn't mean it's not torture."

Antonia glanced up from her position almost between Camila's legs with a raised eyebrow and found Camila looking back at her with a smile. That expression soon turned into a lip bite and a moan when Antonia grazed the exposed skin over her waistband with her tongue again.

Deciding it was time to explore more of the body waiting for her touch, Antonia raised the shirt up Camila's torso, only for it to fly across the room with Camila's help one second later. Antonia couldn't help but let out a laugh at how much she wanted Camila and how good it felt to have her again, this time without reservations and with the prospect of a future.

She kissed every inch of exposed skin. She licked and nibbled everywhere, from Camila's chest to her navel and up again, to the place where her shoulder met her neck, to the edge of her hip, right where her sweatpants had ridden down. With her teeth, she scraped Camila's side up to her rib cage, then grinned at the trail of goose bumps that appeared over her skin.

After kissing her way all over, Antonia came back to Camila's lips. As much as she loved her body, as much as she wanted it, she craved the feel of their mouths against each other more than anything else.

She didn't linger on her lips, moving down to Camila's breasts next and kissing the skin around her nipples with tenderness before sucking hard on the soft flesh, not caring if the act left a mark—or maybe part of her wanted Camila to have that reminder the next day. She sucked hard enough to elicit a reaction but kissed the spot immediately after. Her tongue left a wet trail in its pursuit of Camila's nipple, and once she had it in her mouth, she used her tongue in the same way she had minutes before with her lips.

Camila grew more confident, or more desperate, as the minutes passed. Her hands made Antonia's head their permanent home, pushing and tugging at her hair with the rhythm of Antonia's movements. Antonia let out a mix between a moan and a grunt when the hand on her hair pulled her up for a deep kiss full of tongue and sucking and biting.

"You're driving me to the edge right now. Please. Please, I need more," Camila mumbled against Antonia's mouth.

Antonia smiled and planted a soft peck on the bruised and swollen lips before grabbing Camila's sweatpants and easing them off her, but she still left her underwear on. Just because she intended to listen to Camila's pleas didn't mean she wouldn't make her wait a little more to get what she wanted.

Taking advantage of the thin barrier still covering the area, Antonia buried her head between Camila's legs. She pressed her tongue against Camila's center, positioning it in the exact spot she knew would make Camila unravel. The way her entire body arched in pleasure and both of her hands grabbed Antonia's head to force her to keep pressing on the area told her she'd hit the spot she wanted.

Between the fact that Camila's panties were drenched with her wetness and the way she was squirming underneath her, Antonia let out a loud moan of her own. She alternated between pressing on her center over the panties, grazing the sensitive area with her teeth, and sucking the same spot. No matter what she did, the response from Camila didn't disappoint, from subtle pleas to outright guttural moans that only made Antonia want to tease her more.

Soon Camila was pushing herself against Antonia's mouth, moving up and down in the quest for more stimulation. Antonia didn't mind. Quite the opposite. She enjoyed the increasing signs of desperation. But she also wasn't immune to Camila, and the musky smell hitting her nose and the sweet taste coating her tongue even through the fabric barrier sent a wave of electricity to her lower stomach.

While still kissing through the fabric, she found the edges of Camila's panties and lowered them down her legs. She looked up to find Camila's eyes on her the entire time, and she licked her lips as she held the eye contact. She loved the way Camila's eyes followed each one of her movements.

With the panties out of the way, Antonia had only one minor issue to resolve before diving in fully into pleasuring the woman underneath her. What to do first? She craved the taste of Camila on her tongue, but she also longed to feel her clench around her fingers. Instead of making a choice, she decided to ask the more appropriate person for an answer.

She made her way up again, placing soft kisses alongside Camila's legs and sides until she reached her face.

"How do you want me?" Antonia whispered in her ear.

Camila thought she was going to lose the small vestige of control she had left when Antonia whispered in her ear. *Fuck*. It sounded like such a simple question, but Camila wanted everything. She wanted Antonia to never stop touching her, she wanted to feel her in all the ways possible, and most of all, she wanted the reassurance that this wouldn't be the last time they would be together.

Instead of answering, she grabbed Antonia's face and brought their lips together in a hungry kiss.

"The first thing I want is for you to get rid of some of those clothes. I need to feel your skin," she said, already pulling Antonia's shirt over her head.

Antonia helped her finish the job and stood next to the bed to take off her pants as well. Camila immediately missed the weight and the warmth of her body, but the vision of toned legs being uncovered was enough to distract her. As soon as her pants were off, Antonia lowered herself over her again, leaving open-mouthed kisses on her stomach, up to her chest, and all the way to her neck and ear.

"Anything else you want?" Antonia asked as she scraped the soft skin of the insides of her thighs with her nails, causing Camila to bite her lip to contain the loud moan that wanted to leave her lips.

"Fuck, I want you," she answered. It wasn't articulate, but she struggled to connect words with how Antonia's breath tickled her skin as she kissed her.

When Antonia started heading down in response, Camila reconsidered. She realized what she wanted more than anything else.

"Wait," she exclaimed.

Antonia stopped and looked up at her with curiosity in her eyes. Camila tangled her right hand in Antonia's curls and pulled her up.

"I want you up here with me. I want to see you," she said, her voice so low she wasn't sure if Antonia would hear her. But she had. She reassured her with a nod first and then with a soft kiss that left Camila breathless.

She let out a shudder when Antonia's hand found her center and started rubbing the bundle of nerves between her legs. She did it slowly, grazing it with the tip of her finger, just like Camila liked it.

Camila resisted the urge to close her eyes every time a stroke of Antonia's fingers sent a bolt of electricity from her stomach to her head. It became harder and harder to stay focused as the speed and intensity of Antonia's movements hit her with wave after wave of pleasure, but she fought to keep her eyes open because the raw desire and care reflected in Antonia's eyes made her heart clench and magnified the effects of every touch.

She grasped at Antonia's back and neck, looking for something, anything, to hold on to as she felt control slip away from her. Her ragged breaths increased, as did the rhythm of Antonia's touch. Finally, as the sensations invading her body became too much, she pulled Antonia close for a kiss. Immediately after, her head fell back, eyes shut in ecstasy.

"It's okay, I got you," she heard Antonia say right before the world around her went black for a moment.

As she regained awareness of her surroundings again, Camila felt soft butterfly kisses against the corner of her mouth. It made her smile to feel cared for and protected in Antonia's arms with that simple action. She was so happy and relaxed, like she hadn't been in weeks, but she wasn't ready to let the night end.

She grabbed Antonia's hand and kissed her knuckles one by one before licking each finger. Antonia followed each one of her movements with a glint in her eye and a smirk on her lips.

Camila sat on the bed, opening her legs to allow Antonia to sit between them. The other girl understood her intentions, moving to position herself

JOHANA GAVEZ

in front of her and wrap her legs around Camila's waist.

She leaned down to kiss her first because the urge to kiss Antonia as much as she could had become unbearable since their last conversation. Like all those barely contained feelings needed an escape valve, and kissing Antonia was the only option. Then she moved her hand down between their bodies, sliding two of her fingers inside Antonia and waiting until Antonia mirrored the action.

Camila closed her eyes, overwhelmed by the physical sensations, the pleasure coming from the hand between her legs and how good it felt to have Antonia's warmth surrounding her own fingers. But it was not only that. It was Antonia's eyes looking into hers from inches away that was too much for her to handle.

Instead, she wrapped her free arm around Antonia and brought her closer. She buried her head into the crook of Antonia's neck as she increased the pace of her movements, their panting breaths mixing in a symphony of desire.

Camila collapsed, spent, in Antonia's arms, but the other girl caught her and lowered them both on the bed, placing soft kisses on her temples, her cheeks, and the corners of her mouth. Camila's eyelids grew heavy as Antonia pulled the covers over them. She was

272

lying next to her but still too far away, as if she was afraid of Camila pushing her away if she got too close.

"Hold me," Camila said, closing her eyes.

"Always," she heard in reply as an arm wrapped around her waist and Antonia's head pressed against her shoulder.

Chapter Nineteen

THREE WEEKS. THREE WEEKS of grilling interviews, of answering the same questions over and over again, of the team investigating and questioning every potential link Camila could have to her father's dealings.

Then the team finally cleared Camila to play again.

The same couldn't be said for Coach Medina. Fortunately, his situation didn't involve her, but it didn't take much digging to uncover the fact that he'd been colluding with her father to do all kinds of murky deals on the male teams he'd worked for before joining the Houston Starlight. They fired him and made Coach Megan the new head coach.

Camila had once thought that being on the bench was the worst punishment she could suffer, but having to watch the games from the stands for the duration of her suspension was even worse.

There was only one thing making it all bearable.

Antonia had stayed true to her word and stood by her during the entire ordeal, from training with her after everyone had already left because Camila insisted on practicing free kicks one more time, to cooking her dinner and holding her at night when the days full of questioning got to her.

She would never admit it to Antonia—okay, maybe one day—but she'd been right. Even with the potential of separation looming over them, it was worth it to make the most of the time they had together.

Camila stayed behind in the locker room before her first match after her suspension ended, not sure about the reception of the fans. But Antonia waited for her. She leaned on the doorframe, the start of a grin lifting the corner of her mouth. It was unfair how sexy she looked, especially since Camila couldn't enjoy it thanks to the knot that had been in her stomach for hours now.

She'd missed the end of the regular season, watching and cheering on her teammates from the sidelines. But as thankful as she was to join the team for the playoff semifinals—and even more thankful that Coach Megan had included her as a starter—she'd also never been more nervous in her life. It wasn't a regular match, no matter how much she wanted to pretend it was. There would be so many more eyes on her, and most of all, she didn't want to let her teammates down.

She took a deep breath, thinking back to the words Coach Megan told her the day before: "You worked hard these past few weeks, even though there was no guarantee you'd be able to play. There's nothing better than a hungry player, so you'll be starting the next match. Don't disappoint me."

With the coach's words still resonating in her mind, she gave her shoelaces one last hard squeeze, tying them as tight as possible without cutting off the circulation to her feet. Instead of standing up, she stared at the floor, not able to take the last step necessary to join her teammates.

A pair of green-and-yellow cleats filled her view. The colors were a dead giveaway, but she would have known it was Antonia anyway. She'd grown so used to her presence, to her smell, that she would recognize her with her eyes closed.

"You ready to kick ass today?" Antonia asked.

"I'm just hoping to not embarrass myself, but yeah."

Antonia kneeled in front of her and placed her hand on Camila's thigh. "You're gonna do great. I know it."

Camila nodded, but inside she was still unsure if she'd be able to live up to the occasion. Antonia got up and walked away, then stopped by the door and turned around. She cocked her head and threw Camila that disarming smirk she used to hate but now could admit she loved.

"Come on. I got you," she said.

Camila stood up and jogged the few steps separating them. She grabbed Antonia's hand, and they walked like that all the way through the halls and down the tunnel until they reached their teammates. She was still nervous, but Antonia's words served as a reminder: Just as she hadn't been alone while handling the fallout from her dad's dealings, she wouldn't be alone during the match either.

The first thing Camila noticed when they stepped onto the field was the absence of Antonia's hand over her own. She'd led her from the locker room, through the tunnels, and onto the field silently, but the reassurance of her touch had been enough to calm the raging nerves swirling inside Camila. The second thing she noticed was how imposing the stadium looked. The way it towered over her took her back to her childhood, when she felt so small as she ran around, clinging to her dad and pretending she was the biggest star there could be.

It was not a packed stadium full of roaring fans like in her dreams, but among the faceless small crowd there to support them, she saw the team flag waving in the distance. Little kids wore their shirts with pride, and she even spotted one or two with her last name on it. She took a step, then another, and then another, until her legs stopped weighing her down and she could take off running.

She connected to the earth beneath her feet each time the grass gave way under her cleats' studs. The energy of the ground traveled up her body and filled her with a steadiness she hadn't felt in a long time. As Camila took one last look at the people around her—Antonia, Coach Megan, Liz, and the rest of her teammates—the nerves that had her stomach in knots and her head dizzy soon settled into a barely there pleasant tingle all over her muscles.

For the first time, she would be playing for herself and only herself.

And she'd never been more ready.

During the first minutes, neither team held the ball for more than a few passes. Both squads couldn't break the thick defensive schemes the coaches had opted for in such an important match. Camila sprinted back and forth, helping the midfield recover the ball more than she ran in the opposite direction to break the opposing team's defense. Despite her frustration, she knew that working for the good of the team was more important, and if they kept the pressure up, they would have a chance.

It was almost the end of the first half when López recovered a ball in the midfield and passed it to Antonia. Before the ball even touched Antonia's feet, Camila ran diagonal to her, trying to show her she was ready to break their opponent's defense if she gave her a long pass. As she expected, Antonia understood her intentions. She sent a precise pass to the edge of the penalty area that took the defenders by surprise. The goalkeeper, realizing Camila would have free range to shoot if she caught the ball, ran forward to get to it before she did. Camila pushed harder, willing her muscles to run faster than she ever had. When it seemed like she would collide with the goalkeeper and lose the chance to score, she slid down and kicked under the ball with the tip of her foot to send it spiraling over the helpless goalkeeper.

She watched in slow motion as the ball flew over the goalkeeper's head right before their bodies crashed into each other. From her spot on the ground, she followed the ball's path, a smile spreading over her face when it became obvious the ball had only one possible destination—the back of the net. Unfortunately, in her effort to win the ball, she didn't hit it with as much power and intention as she would have liked. One valiant defender pushed it out with a sliding kick right as the ball grazed the goal line, sending it to a corner kick.

Camila cursed under her breath at missing the chance to take the lead in the game, but she got up with a spring in her step that she usually wouldn't have. Despite not scoring, she smiled because it would have been a beautiful goal if she'd made it. When normally she would have been angry at the missed opportunity, this time she was ecstatic at having the chance to play and almost score.

Antonia bumped her shoulder as she ran past her. "Well played. We'll get the next one."

Camila smiled. "Yeah, we will," she said to Antonia's retreating back, not sure if she heard her.

Antonia took care of the corner kick that resulted from Camila's almost goal. Despite her precise touch and the way the ball flew above their heads at the perfect height and fell in the center of the penalty area, the vicious, close one-on-one defense prevented any of them from winning the position. The goalkeeper grabbed the ball, and they returned to their back-and-forth, their give-and-take, with few options to score for either side.

Antonia drank a large gulp of Gatorade as she listened to the instructions for the second half. Coach Megan asked her to fall back a little, to come from behind, down the wings, and move freely from right to left to surprise the other team and break their defensive stronghold. She also asked Camila to move several steps back, so she was closer to Antonia. This would ideally create more opportunities for passes between the two of them since the few chances they had to score in the first half were all thanks to them. The only thing capable of breaking the almost impenetrable defense of the other team was Antonia's quickness and precise touch mixed with Camila's strength and ability to anticipate.

"I know you're still a little rusty, Sánchez, but we need to exploit that connection you have on the field with Carvalho," Coach Megan said as she walked from one end of the locker room to the other. "López, you've been doing great on defense, and I need you to stay strong there but also cover the space Carvalho leaves when she moves around like I asked."

There was more to the talk, and Antonia should have paid attention to all of it, but as soon as the coach mentioned her connection with Camila, her eyes wandered over to her. Camila's eyes were drawn together in that furrowed brow Antonia had seen repeatedly in the past, except she wasn't the cause of it this time. Camila watched the coach, her attention never wavering, while Antonia stared at her with a smile on her face.

Sharing the pitch with Camila had become one of her favorite things, and in this match, they were more in sync than ever. It was like Antonia knew what Camila was going to do before she did it.

She forced her gaze away from Camila just in time to hear the tail end of the coach's speech.

"We got it, Coach," Antonia said with a wink. She looked in Camila's direction.

As if on cue, a light blush colored Camila's face in the most adorable way.

"Oh, I'm sure you and your *connection* got it," López replied. The way she emphasized the word "connection" earned her a sharp elbow to the ribs.

The Houston Starlight started the second half with a frenetic pace, attacking relentlessly and putting the pressure on the other team. They had at least four corner kicks with headshots that almost looked in until the goalkeeper pushed them out with the tips of her fingers.

It was frustrating to feel so close, the scream of "goal" burning in their throats, only to be put out at the last minute. But Antonia knew they needed to keep going, keep trying, and eventually they would break through the defense and score.

As time ticked by and the coach screamed instructions from the edge of the pitch, it seemed as if the net on their rival's side became smaller. It was the only explanation for the way their shots never made it into the net after so many close calls.

The fourth referee had just raised the sign showing an additional four minutes of play when the ball got to Antonia's feet right outside the penalty area. She lifted her head to survey the space around her, only to find it crowded with at least eight members of the opposite team. It was clear they were aiming to keep the score at zero until the extra time. She couldn't find an obvious option for a pass, so she positioned the ball to her left and tried on her own. The powerful shot passed between the defenders and over the goalkeeper's hand to hit the post, making it tremble and sending the ball out of the pitch.

"Bad luck, but good try," López said, patting Antonia on the shoulder as she ran past.

With one minute left until the end of regulation, a bad rejection from the other team gave the Starlight a side throw-in near the opposing team's area. López took it, using all her strength to send the ball flying to the middle of the penalty area, almost as if it were a corner kick. Antonia wasn't sure what happened because it all became a tangle of legs moving around with everyone trying to kick the ball. Camila got it, and one second later, to everyone's confusion, it was inside the goal.

The entire team screamed and rushed to jump on Camila, including the players sitting on the bench. Amid the chaos, Antonia ended up pressed against her. With all their teammates surrounding them and hiding them from the cameras, Antonia took the chance to leave a quick peck on Camila's cheek.

"I told you we would do it," she said.

When the sea of people cleared, Antonia's eyes landed on the bright yellow flag that the line judge was holding a few feet away.

They had nullified the goal.

Camila and Antonia led the rain of protests against the referee, to no avail. No matter what they told him, he insisted there had been a hand that invalidated the goal.

Two minutes later, regulation ended with the score tied at zero. The extra time period ended up in the same way. They would decide their fate on penalty kicks.

Antonia took the first penalty. She kicked the ball high and strong to the right-hand corner to score their first goal. López, Brown, Young, and Camila scored theirs too, as did their rivals. With the score at 5-4, tension rose in the air. The team watched from the middle of the pitch, arms all around each other as the last kicker from the other team prepared to take their shot.

Antonia held her breath, watching the ball roll on the grass toward the right-hand corner of the net. Their goalkeeper guessed the correct side, but the kick was strong and well placed. Just as it looked like the shot would go in, their goalie stretched and touched the ball at the last second with her fingertips, giving the Houston Starlight the win.

Chapter Twenty

BREATH, CAMILA'S MUSCLES ACHED FROM a mix of the strenuous semifinal and the after-game celebration she had with Antonia once they got home. Her gaze wandered to the exposed tanned legs that had suddenly moved to rest on top of hers. Though Antonia had been sound asleep until seconds before, she now stirred and moved around in that half-unconscious, half-aware state right before waking up. She snuggled closer.

A soft smile appeared on Camila's lips. The best decision she'd made was to stop pushing Antonia away. She really couldn't ask for more. Well, maybe when they got to play in the finals in one week, she wanted to score for the team. But even if she didn't, she would be happy.

Antonia's fingers traced light patterns on her leg, alerting Camila to the fact that she had woken up. She didn't seem in a rush to get up, and Camila wasn't either. Antonia wrapped her arms around her, bringing her even closer, and planted pecks along the edge of Camila's collarbone, then up her shoulders and neck. Every time the soft lips touched her skin, Camila hummed in appreciation. She turned around and buried her head in the crook of Antonia's neck.

"Can we stay in bed all day?" Camila mumbled, lips hovering over Antonia's skin. She was so focused on watching how the smooth surface broke into goose bumps, she almost missed Antonia's answer.

"I don't see why we can't. We have the day off, after all, and I can't think of a better place to spend the day than in bed with you." She kissed the top of Camila's head. "Coach wanted us to rest, but maybe I'll just go easy on you. Can't risk an injury right before the finals."

Camila scoffed. "Maybe you're just making up excuses because you're not up to my level. Can't keep up."

"Oh, is that what you think," Antonia said, grinning as she rolled over to hold Camila's hands up above her head.

Camila felt the movement all the way down to her core. Heat pooled in her lower abdomen, though it wasn't the only part of her body that reacted to

Antonia. Her chest tightened, and warmth traveled from her head to her stomach, but it was a different type of warmth. Not the intense one born out of lust, but a softer, gentler kind that spread through her entire being from the inside out. The feeling started from her toes, made its way up her legs and torso, passed through her chest and her heart, then ended on the tip of her tongue. To stop the words she could feel forming on her lips from escaping, she leaned in and captured Antonia's mouth in a kiss. She wasn't ready to say those three little words. She wasn't even ready to think about them and accept what they meant. As long as she didn't say them, as long as they didn't cross her mind, the possibility of going back still existed. But the longer she spent in Antonia's arms, the less she wanted to imagine a life without her embrace.

Her tongue teased Antonia's mouth while her hands grasped her thighs. The phone rang in the distance. She ignored it, not interested in finding out who it was, until Antonia moved away from her and reached over her head to retrieve the phone from the nightstand.

She would've been mad at her for picking up if she wasn't so distracted by the fact that Antonia had sat on top of her, spread thighs pressing into Camila's hip while she talked on the phone. Camila traced patterns along the inside of Antonia's thigh. The brief twitches caused by each one of her touches filled her with satisfaction. She started on the outside of Antonia's legs, but her fingers soon moved upward and inward, closer and closer to Antonia's center, making her squirm a little more the closer Camila got to the sensitive area.

She knew she was treading in dangerous waters, but the movement became hypnotizing, and even more so when she noticed the way Antonia's breath hitched when the ghost of her touch hovered over that little spot that would make her unravel.

The wetness coating Antonia's center became obvious against her bare skin, and Camila couldn't help but dip her finger into the glistening fold she'd been teasing so far. She heard a sharp intake of breath before Antonia grabbed her wrist. There was no actual force behind it, but the action got Camila to stop. She looked up to find dilated pupils staring back at her.

"You're playing dirty," Antonia mouthed.

Camila relented, knowing she was right, but the urge to touch Antonia was still present. Instead, she sat up to plant soft kisses along her neck as she spoke.

"Yeah, that's awesome," Antonia said into the phone. "Send it my way, and I'll get you the signed contract back as soon as possible."

The words stopped Camila in her tracks. She hadn't been paying attention to the conversation, but the memories of their previous discussion came back stronger than ever. She tried to control the rising uneasiness in her stomach. Gone were the butterflies, which had been replaced with an urge to throw up.

"What was that about?"

The way Antonia's body tensed at the question was all the answer Camila needed. She let out a shaky chuckle and pushed Antonia off her.

"Camila, wait," Antonia said as Camila walked around the room and started putting on the discarded pieces of clothes.

She didn't listen. She didn't turn around to look at Antonia, and she didn't stop getting dressed. The only thing she wanted was to run away before the tears already prickling at the edges of her eyes fell.

"Wait," Antonia said again. She'd moved closer to Camila and had a hand on her shoulder.

Camila stopped moving at the touch, rooted in place, all the fight she'd felt a minute before now gone. Antonia pushed her shoulders until she turned around. They stood face-to-face, only inches apart. Standing so close and looking into those beautiful brown eyes became too much for Camila to handle, and the tears she'd fought so hard to contain were soon unleashed.

Antonia wiped away the trail of tears with her thumb. "I never lied to you." She kissed the left side of her face, cleaning away the tears with her lips. "You knew I was going to leave." She repeated the action on the other side of her face.

Anger rose inside Camila, replacing the pain. "You said you were considering it. I guess it's on me for thinking you would care enough about me to stay."

"I do care about you," Antonia said, and Camila wanted to believe her. "This is an incredible opportunity. It would be great for my career, and it would be great for my family." She took a deep breath, and Camila braced herself for the rejection she knew was coming. "I want to have you in my life, but I also need to do what's best for me. Those two things can exist at the same time."

Camila wanted to be upset. She wanted to get angry and yell and push her away, but she didn't have the energy. She wanted Antonia, and she didn't want to lose her when she had only just started to have her. The realization scared her, but she was tired of shutting Antonia out. She already knew what would happen if she did. She also knew it wasn't fair to ask Antonia to give up on her dreams because of her. If it was her in Antonia's position, she wouldn't give up on her own dreams for anybody.

"Is this it? Are we done?" Camila asked, trying to keep her sobs under control. "You give me the best days of my life and then you walk away?"

"Do you want it to be over?"

She hated the fact that Antonia had turned the question back on her. But she understood why she'd done it. It was always Camila pushing her away, so of course she expected her to do the same again this time.

"You're leaving," Camila answered.

"That's not what I asked."

Camila clenched her jaw. No, she didn't want it to be over, yet still, she couldn't get herself to say the words. She could handle the rejection if Antonia left by pretending she never wanted her in the first place, but admitting out loud that wasn't the case left her without an excuse to protect herself. But then, what was the point of lying when the truth was obvious to both of them? Antonia had given care and affection to Camila when she needed it most. The least she could do was give honesty back.

"I want to be with you." The words almost got caught up in her throat, but she pushed them out. "I don't know how it happened, since you annoyed me for like half of the time we've known each other."

She held her breath, waiting for Antonia's answer, hoping her lame attempt at humor worked to hide the weight of the words she'd just said.

"You annoyed me too." Antonia winked. "If we both want this, then we'll find a way." Antonia cradled her face and kissed her gently.

The tears that had almost dried up started flowing down Camila's face again. "How?"

"There are phones, there are flights, there's a long off-season. I want to be with you, and you want to be with me. Why not try?"

It sounded so simple when she said it like that. Camila doubted they would survive more than a month apart, but seeing Antonia's soft smile directed at her, she knew she had to give them at least the opportunity to try. She wasn't ready to lose Antonia so soon.

"What are we going to do?"

Antonia sighed. "Well, first we are going to get back in bed and spend our day off naked. Then we're going to play in the finals and win them. After that, I'm planning a full night of celebration, and then we'll take it day by day while we figure it out."

Antonia tied her boots with a heavy heart. This would be the last time she wore the Houston Starlight uniform. She knew that joining the Olympique Lyonnais in France was the right call, the best for her and her brother, but her heart still grew heavy with saudades of the life she'd built in Houston over the last year.

A bump to the shoulder made her look up.

Camila offered her hand to help her stand. "You look pensive. That's usually my job."

Antonia forced a smile. "Just pregame jitters."

"Really? Weren't you the one who once told me to not take things so seriously? To go out and have fun?"

"That sounds like me, yeah. But this match is different." She smiled. "You're right, though. We'll go out, have fun, and score some goals."

Camila nodded. "Let's do it."

Antonia stepped onto the pitch more determined to win than ever, and it seemed like the rest of the team was also as focused as she was. They were playing as a unit, in perfect sync. Like they were one mind, always connected, with no need to talk or look at each other to know where a teammate would be. They attacked relentlessly from the start of the match while their opponents scrambled to keep them at bay.

Antonia used the right wing to destabilize. She ran down the band, almost to the edge of the pitch, before throwing a long pass to the middle of the penalty area to try to get a headshot, or leave the defenders behind to find an angle to shoot. So far, either a well-timed save by the goalkeeper or a last-minute intervention by a defender had kept them from screaming "goal," but after a failed attack by the opposing team, she ran in a counterattack. It was López, Camila, and her against only two defenders.

López passed the ball to her, knowing that with her speed, she could take advantage of the opening. Antonia found herself alone in front of the goalkeeper, who ran toward her in a desperate attempt to stop the inevitable. Right as the goalkeeper threw herself at Antonia's feet, she saw out of the corner of her eye that Camila had arrived from behind to join the action. In a swift movement, Antonia passed the ball to Camila, who easily won the position over the defender to score on the open goal.

She wasn't sure who screamed harder, Camila or her. She didn't remember who ran toward whom. She only knew that Camila ended up in her arms. The rest of the team soon joined them, but for an instant, it felt like it was only the two of them on the pitch.

"Have fun, score some goals. Maybe you were onto something," Camila told her as she ran away from her.

The first half ended with that lone goal as their only advantage, but Antonia felt confident about their prospects. They were in control of the game, and in only forty-five more minutes, they would run around with a trophy in their hands.

At least that was what she expected when they jumped onto the pitch again, but she didn't count on a string of mistakes on defense costing them the tie.

"Fuck," Camila mumbled at her.

"It's okay. We got this," Antonia replied.

It was easier said than done, but a perfectly placed corner kick from Antonia and a precise headshot by Camila gave them the lead again with five minutes to go.

The last few minutes of the match were a stressful give-and-take, but this time their defense held up. They maintained the advantage until the end to win the championship.

The final whistle unleashed a wave of screams so loud it was impossible to tell which ones came from the crowd in the stands and which ones were from her teammates. But among the confusion and excitement, Antonia and Camila found each other. Camila melted into her body, and Antonia didn't hesitate to wrap her arms around her and hold her tight.

"We won!" Camila screamed.

"We did, and you were the MVP," Antonia said, nudging her shoulder.

"I wasn't. You practically made the goals. I just pushed them in."

"No. You deserve all the credit." Antonia gazed at Camila with all the care and love she could put in one simple look, hoping it was enough to convey how much she meant the words.

"You were right when you said we would make a good team. We do," Camila relented. "Too bad this is the last time we'll play together," she added, her voice sounding smaller with every word.

Antonia wished she could kiss the sadness away, but in the middle of the pitch, with their teammates running around celebrating and thousands of people cheering them on in the stands, the only thing she could do was squeeze Camila's hand.

"We'll still be a team, only a different kind."

Camila nodded, and Antonia pulled her as she ran toward the rest of their teammates. "Come on. Let's celebrate!" she yelled over her shoulder.

Chapter Twenty-One

ANTONIA DROPPED THE KEYS three times while trying to open the door to their apartment. It was late, and both of them were tipsy after the amount of champagne that had been passed around the locker room for hours after the championship. They drank, they sang, they showered each other in champagne. Camila even kissed her in front of the entire team, earning them a chorus of whistles.

They stumbled around the apartment on their way to the bedroom, giggling and tripping over the furniture. Antonia helped Camila out of her shirt and pants as they walked, and then took off her own clothes until she was clad in only her underwear by the time they made it to the bedroom.

She led Camila to the bed with a mix of kisses and subtle touches. She pushed her and crawled on top of her with a lot less grace than usual. The covers got tangled up with her legs, and she almost headbutted Camila by accident while wrestling them off. When she liberated herself and resumed her journey, Camila had her eyes closed, and her breathing was evening out. Antonia kissed her forehead and circled her arms around her.

"I think alcohol makes me tired," Camila said, burying her head into Antonia's neck.

Antonia planted another kiss on her forehead. "Let's go to sleep."

She woke up the next morning with a slight headache and Camila wrapped around her body. The embrace invited her to stay in bed, to lose herself in the warm air tickling her neck with each of Camila's breaths. She stayed, aware that there was not much time before she had to leave for France to join her new team and that when she did, waking up in each other's arms would stop being an everyday occurrence. She basked in the happiness and calm that the position brought her for what felt like hours before extracting herself carefully to go make breakfast.

By the time she finished making her famous candied strawberry pancakes, Camila was still sleeping. She put the spread of food on a tray and skipped toward the bedroom, set the tray on the bedside table, and placed small kisses along Camila's legs, arms, and shoulders until she stirred awake.

Camila opened one eye and left the other closed. "Hey."

Antonia leaned down and kissed her. "Good morning," she said, then kissed her again. "I brought you breakfast."

Camila looked back at her with a lazy smile on her face. "What's the special occasion?"

"It's your reward for being the MVP in yesterday's match, and I enjoy taking care of you."

"You're spoiling me. I won't know what to do when you leave." Camila laughed, but the smile soon disappeared.

Antonia sat on the bed, putting the breakfast tray between them. "No need to think about that yet. We've still got time."

"How much?" Camila asked, looking into her eyes.

They'd avoided the topic for the most part since their last conversation about it, not wanting to bring the mood down with a reminder of her moving away.

Antonia lowered her gaze. "The team expects me to join them in two weeks."

Camila sighed but said nothing else.

"Hey, I'll FaceTime you and tell you how to make breakfast." She used her finger to raise Camila's head and make her look at her. "How about that?"

"Can I just go to IHOP and FaceTime you from there? You know that cooking is not my thing." Camila smiled, but Antonia knew her well enough to notice how it didn't reach her eyes.

Antonia wished there was something she could do to make the prospect of leaving less daunting, but she knew that words were useless. No matter how many promises she made or how much she intended to keep them, they both knew this was uncharted territory. They would only know for real how it would affect them once they went through it.

Still, she used the strength of their physical connection to convey what she couldn't get herself to say. Her thumb traveled from Camila's chin to her lips and back again, only to be replaced by her lips in the end.

She took Camila's lower lip between her own and sucked on it for a few seconds, only letting go to switch to her upper lip. The kiss remained slow and gentle. They kept their foreheads pressed together long after the kiss ended, noses touching, their breaths mixing as one.

Antonia opened her eyes after what felt like an eternity of basking in each other's presence. "We'll make it work."

Camila nodded and buried her head in Antonia's chest as if to protect herself from the reality of her leaving. Antonia wasn't sure how they were going to get through it—she only knew that as long as they both wanted to be together, they would find a way.

For the next two weeks, Camila tried her best to ignore the doomsday clock that hung over their heads, but the weight inside her chest grew heavier each day. She let Antonia hold her every night and wake her up with butterfly kisses every morning. Antonia took her out to dinner, to an Astros game, and to dance all night at a club. They pretended they were just two people dating and having fun together like anybody else.

They tried their hardest to forget that the inevitable was bound to happen, until it became impossible to ignore any longer with how the open suitcase in Antonia's room acted as a giant neon sign reminding them of the fact that she was leaving in less than a day.

Camila sat on the edge of the bed. The still empty suitcase rested next to her while Antonia rummaged through her clothes in the closet. Camila glared at the suitcase, as if it were the one at fault for Antonia leaving. She wanted to push it away, hide it. Maybe if she kept the suitcase out of sight, if she stopped Antonia from packing, the goodbye would never come.

But she knew that wasn't how it worked; Antonia would leave no matter what she said or wanted.

It was easier to be upset at the suitcase for preventing her from pushing Antonia onto the bed and kissing every part of her body one last time than to be upset at Antonia for choosing her career over her. Or to be upset at herself for not being able to tell Antonia how much she cared, how much it hurt to see her leave. Instead, she kept pretending everything was okay. She helped Antonia fold her clothes and place them neatly until all her belongings were inside and ready to cross the ocean the next day.

Camila was lost in her own thoughts, staring at a fixed point on the wall, when Antonia grabbed her hand and raised it to her lips. She kissed her knuckles with a softness that made Camila's heart clench.

"I'll call you as soon as I get settled," Antonia said, then kissed her hand again. "And Arantxa said she'll show us around when you come visit. We can go to Spain and Italy."

Camila nodded. "That sounds great." She leaned down to kiss Antonia, a long, languid kiss that tingled on her lips long after it was over. "Are you going to miss me?" she asked. "Are you going to feel saudades of me?" she added, remembering the conversation they'd had what now seemed like a lifetime ago.

Antonia kissed her and rested her forehead against hers. "I haven't left yet, and I already estou com saudades de você."

Silence settled over them. Antonia held Camila's face, tracing every corner with her thumb like she'd done so many times before. They stared into each other's eyes, as if both of them willed their gazes to speak for them. Camila knew what she wanted to say and what she longed to hear. That longing may have made her read what she wanted to read, but when she stared into Antonia's eyes, there was so much care, so much softness, and, dare she say it, so much love in those bright brown pupils that she never wanted to look away.

She wondered what her own eyes showed. Probably her sadness, her barely contained longing for another day, another hour, another minute with Antonia.

Camila bit her lip, realizing the love she'd been craving to see in Antonia's eyes had been in front of her all along. She thought back to the endless nights curled against her body. The way Antonia held her until she fell asleep while she whispered reassuring words against her hair. She remembered the passion and need in those stolen, drunken kisses when they went out to party, but she also felt the ghost of a barely there peck full of warmth she'd received more than once from those same lips.

There hadn't been a big declaration. Antonia had never said the words, but Camila was sure Antonia felt the same way she did. Maybe this time it was her turn to take a leap, to be the first one to put herself out there. Normally, it would terrify her. She'd never exposed herself, not knowing for sure what answer she'd get back. But Antonia was leaving, and while yes, they'd promised each other to try, there were no guarantees. Camila didn't want to spend weeks or months with the words stuck in her throat, unable to say them with Antonia's hands between her own and her lips within reach. Or even worse, she didn't want to stay silent and maybe lose her chance to say it if they didn't survive the distance.

And maybe she should have planned it better or tried to make it more romantic, but things with Antonia had always happened like that—in the spur of the moment. Like an unstoppable force she could never control.

Camila took a deep breath and repeated the gesture Antonia had done with her so many times. She brought Antonia's hand up to her lips and kissed her knuckles, taking the chance to inhale the essence of her skin before raising her gaze to look into her eyes.

"I love you," she said, and despite her best effort, her voice broke at the end.

Antonia smiled at her and raised her hand to cup Camila's face. Camila closed her eyes, leaning into the caress, not even caring that Antonia had said nothing back yet. She didn't open her eyes again until the soft pressure of Antonia's lips against her cheek made her realize she was crying.

The more Antonia kissed away her tears, moving her lips along her cheeks and chin, the more tears Camila shed, until Antonia had to kiss her eyelids to stay ahead of the tears.

"I love you too," Antonia said, and she kissed away another one. "I love you too, and we'll make it work."

Camila nodded, finally able to stop the tears because she believed her.

Epilogue

CAMILA MISSED ANTONIA FROM the minute she left, and she struggled to keep her voice even and her desire to beg her to come back at bay every time they talked on the phone. Not because she was afraid of being vulnerable, which wasn't the reason for once, but because despite how much Antonia told her that she missed her, it was also obvious how happy she was on her new team, in her new country, in her new home, and Camila didn't want to do anything to bring her down.

She smiled when Antonia gave her a complete tour of the quaint little apartment the team had rented for her in downtown Lyon, and she wolf-whistled when Antonia modeled the Lyon uniform for her—white with stripes of red and blue—before her official presentation to the press.

Camila wasn't skilled enough at hiding the layer of sadness underneath the genuine happiness she had for all the good things happening to Antonia. Or maybe Antonia just knew her that well. Of course she did, and of course she would call her out on it.

"I don't like seeing you sad," Antonia said one day out of the blue while they had their weekly movie night.

"I'm not sad," Camila replied. "I'm not, I swear," she added when Antonia raised an eyebrow. "I just miss you a lot, that's all."

Camila watched, mesmerized, as Antonia bit her lip. The action distracted her so much that she almost missed her next words.

"Have you ever thought about playing in Europe?"

Camila frowned in thought for a second. "Going from the NCAA to a local team was always the plan. I never thought of Europe as a possibility. I mean, I wasn't even sure any team would want me here."

"You scored the two goals that won your team the championship of one of the most important leagues in the world, and the USWNT asked you to join the team for their next tournament. I think if you were interested, you'd be able to find some options."

The idea took a minute to sink in, but when it did, Camila couldn't stop her heart from racing inside her chest. Not at the idea of playing on a European team, but at the possibility of being closer to Antonia and the implication that Antonia wanted her closer too.

"It never occurred to me, but there's nothing keeping me here. My dad handled my negotiations. We never had a contract or anything, but he always decided what he thought was best, and I never questioned him." Camila paused, lowering her gaze at the memory of the disappointment her dad had turned out to be. "Maybe I should look into it. I need to get a new manager first, but I wouldn't hate it."

Antonia beamed. "I can tell Arantxa to call you. No pressure."

As soon as Antonia planted the idea in her head, Camila couldn't stop thinking about it. She tried to manage her expectations, since there was no guarantee a team would want her, but the possibility of being closer to Antonia had her heart beating a hundred miles per hour.

As promised, Arantxa called her a couple of days later, and they hit it off right away. It was interesting to work with someone who wasn't family for the first time in her life, but it was hard to not trust Arantxa. After Camila signed a contract with her, it didn't take long for the offers to start coming in.

She'd allowed herself to dream about the possibility of playing for Lyon too. After so much complaining, she'd gotten used to sharing the field with Antonia, and their last games were proof of how well they played together. But of course, she knew that was probably too much to ask for.

She received an offer from FC Barcelona and another from Paris Saint-Germain. Both teams would be a great opportunity for her as a player, but being only a few hours away from Antonia was too tempting to pass up, even if it meant playing for a rival team in the same country.

Camila had never planned for the future she ended up living. She always thought her life was in the United States, showing her worth in the NWSL. She never thought about leaving, about making somewhere else a home. But when she thought about it, the houses she shared with her parents growing up never felt like home. She wasn't even sure she knew what it meant to feel warm and safe, like everyone always said a home should feel, until Antonia left and their apartment felt as cold and lifeless as her parents' house. She decided she'd rather leave and build a proper home in France with Antonia by her side. A place where she didn't feel alone, even if there was no one else home, because the atmosphere would be full of warmth and happy memories.

She smiled at the thought as she made her way from the plane to the airport gate, where Antonia waited for her. Camila had no time to react before Antonia had her arms wrapped around her and her lips resting on her cheek.

"Welcome to France, babe."

Camila nuzzled her head in the crook of Antonia's neck and inhaled her intoxicating aroma with a deep breath that filled her lungs and her soul. She rested her head on Antonia's shoulder and they held hands all the way to her new apartment, not needing to look out the car window to take in the sights of the city because the only thing that mattered was right there next to her.

When they arrived, she didn't care that it was impossible for Antonia to open the door to Camila's new apartment with how her hands roamed over Antonia's body and how she kept kissing her desperately. She'd been deprived of Antonia's taste for too long, and she didn't want to wait any longer.

"Babe, slow down," Antonia breathed out.

Camila was ready to get lost in Antonia right there in the middle of the hallway when the door in front of them opened.

"Seemed like you needed some help there," said an unfamiliar voice. A handsome man with sandy blond hair and the same kindness in his eyes as Antonia stood next to the open door.

When the haze of arousal left her mind, Camila realized it was Antonia's brother, Leo.

"Hi!" she said.

"Hi there, new sis," he answered, and he leaned forward to wrap her in a hug that felt almost as welcoming as Antonia's arms.

He grabbed her suitcase and led them inside, where the sweet smell of food reminded Camila that she hadn't had a proper meal in several hours.

As she watched Leo cook and Antonia try to steal a taste of it while he wasn't looking, Camila felt a smile spread over her face. This was what a home was supposed to feel like. Even though Antonia and Leo wouldn't be there tomorrow once they had to leave to live their own lives, she knew she didn't need to be afraid. Their presence would linger in every corner of the house, and eventually, they would come back.

As Antonia had told her, they would make it work.

Bonus Epilogue

END GOAL

RIGHT BEFORE THE MOST important game of her life, Camila sat alone on the locker room bench. The rest of the team was on the way to the field, but she needed a few more minutes on her own. It was a habit she'd started by accident back when she wanted to hide from the world and keep everyone at arm's-length. She'd changed a lot since those days, at least she thought so. But she couldn't bring herself to let go of this one tradition, habit, superstition—whatever you wanted to call it. She needed time with no one around to center her mind and push down the inevitable surge of pre-match jitters.

She closed her eyes and took one, two, three deep breaths. An image formed in her mind. She pictured lifting the World Cup Trophy, raising it high above her head and kissing it. When she opened her eyes again, insecurity had subsided enough to give space to conviction and purpose. She ran out of the locker room, sure tonight would be the night she made her biggest dream come true.

Her teammates on the U.S. Women's National Team (USWNT) stood outside the tunnel in a straight line, ready to jump on the field. Next to them, a similar group clad in the bright green and yellow uniforms Camila had become so familiar with over the years also waited. A loud cackling laugh she would recognize anywhere pulled Camila's attention towards the Brazilian team. Antonia stood a couple of steps ahead of her, chatting animatedly with some of her teammates and Camila couldn't help but stare. It wouldn't be the first time they played against each other. They'd done it plenty of times after moving to France to play professional soccer and ending up on opposing teams. Antonia playing for the Olympique Lyonnais and Camila for Paris Saint-Germain. It wasn't even the first time they would face the other with their national teams, but no match was as important as the one they were about to play.

Camila had dreamed about winning the World Cup since she was a kid. Having the possibility so close excited and terrified her in equal measure. She'd been able to keep her cool for the duration of the tournament by focusing all her energy on the next game, but ever since the referee blew the whistle signaling the end of their semifinal, the reality of being in the final game of the most important tournament in the world overwhelmed her. Tightness was ever-present in her stomach, so much so that not even Antonia's jokes the night before had helped turn them away. The feeling had only increased the closer it got to the match, now she felt like she would throw up at any minute.

She forced another deep breath into her lungs, only to have the wind knocked out of her a second later when Antonia's brown eyes meet her own. The smile and wink from Antonia did nothing to ease her nerves; her heart beat harder in her chest and her stomach flipped around even more. She tried to smile back, but it must have come out as a grimace instead, because Antonia furrowed her eyebrows in reaction. As the teams started walking out, Antonia let her teammates pass her until she ended up next to Camila.

"I thought you'd look happier right before your dream game," Antonia mumbled, leaning closer.

"I can't believe you're so relaxed," Camila answered through gritted teeth. Their relationship wasn't a secret, but she still didn't want people overhearing them. She didn't want anyone but Antonia to know how nervous she was.

"Why wouldn't I be?" Antonia replied, with a smug smirk, which used to infuriate Camila so much, firmly in place.

Nowadays, Camila found the smirk and accompanying smugness sexy most of the time, but with how stressed she was at the moment, annoyance flickered, reminiscent of old times, before she pushed it down. This was Antonia. Positive and laid back. The perfect balance to Camila's own tendency to worry and stress about the smallest things. Even after being together for so long, it still amazed her how easily confidence came to Antonia, while she struggled with the voice in the back of her mind telling her she wasn't good enough.

"Are you never afraid of failing?" she mumbled.

She didn't expect Antonia to hear her. But she did. Antonia grabbed her arm and held her behind as the rest of their respective teams walked out on the field. The protest died on her lips when her eyes landed on Antonia's face. A soft smile and eyes full of warmth touched Camila.

"Not winning today is not failing." Antonia glanced to her right, to the spot where the tunnel they were going through ended, and the field opened. "You're a world-class football player. One of the stars of your national team, just like you always wanted, and you have been successfully playing in Europe for years now. This game doesn't define you."

Camila nodded and swallowed the ball of emotions settling in her throat and threatening to spill out through her eyes. Antonia always knew what to say to quench her doubts. She had to fight the urge to lean down and kiss Antonia senseless. That would have to wait, but she grabbed Antonia's hand and squeezed it, hoping that would show her how much her words meant. Antonia squeezed Camila's hand back.

"You know what the best part is about both of us being on the final?" Antonia asked.

"That I get to beat your ass and rub it for the rest of our lives?"

"Keep dreaming." Antonia scoffed. "The best part is that no matter what, one of us will win and even if we lose, we get to be happy about the other."

Camila smiled. She was almost ashamed to admit she hadn't thought of it that way until then, but now that Antonia said it, she knew it was true. She didn't want to lose but if she did, she would be so happy for Antonia and would celebrate her success as if it was her own.

"You're right." Camila turned around, ready to jog away to join her teammates. She glanced at Antonia one last time before leaving. "Thank you," she said and took off toward the field.

She loved Antonia and watching her play had become a pleasure, even when she was her rival. It also worried her how easily Antonia broke the USWNT defense and how close she'd been to scoring in the fifteen minutes since the game started, but when she wasn't stressing about her team falling behind, Camila had to admit Antonia's technique and speed were a sight to behold. That didn't stop Camila from sliding down to steal the ball from Antonia, causing her to stumble on the grass. She loved Antonia, but she didn't want her to score and put Brazil in the lead.

"Sorry," she mumbled, and offered her hand to Antonia to help her get up.

Antonia ran away from her as soon as she was up. "No, you're not," she said over her shoulder, but the edges of her lips pulled upwards in a restrained smile.

Camila looked at her lover's retreating form for a couple of extra seconds. She would have stared at her for longer if not for the task at hand. As attractive as Antonia was, as much as she enjoyed looking at her, Camila was still determined to win the game. For that to happen, she needed to focus.

The match was a fast-paced encounter. The Brazilian team attacked relentlessly. Each time they got the ball, they used a long pass or the speed of their wingers to reach their area, and they would either try to lift the ball to the penalty area or attempt to filter a precise pass between the defenders to set up one of their forwards one-on-one against the goalie. They succeeded several times. The only reason the score was still 0-0 was the quick reflexes of the USWNT goalkeeper. The US team had also had their chances to score, but they were fewer and far between.

On a quick counterattack after another save by their goalkeeper, Camila and her teammates got their best chance at scoring. The goal kick passed the middle of the field and landed at the feet of their captain, Stephanie Brown, with only two Brazilian defenders in her way. Camila took off running and joined the offensive, along with two other teammates. First to reach the penalty area, she was right on time to receive a pass from Brown. She intended to hit the ball as soon as she got it, to take away the possibility of the Brazilian defenders reaching her, but right when her boot was about to connect with the ball, a defender aggressively tackled and sent her to the ground. Camila grabbed her leg in pain, but mostly, she was pissed. She'd been so close to scoring.

The referee signaled the penalty kick after the obvious fault. It was a slight comfort to know even if she didn't score, they would get a chance to take the lead. Brown, as team captain, would take the shot. Camila stood at the edge of the penalty area and waited eagerly to take any rebounds if the Brazilian goalkeeper stopped the shot.

Camila focused on the one person standing between her US team and the possibility of a goal: Giovanna Guimarães. She gritted her teeth at the sight of Giovanna jumping around the goal line with her arms stretched out to distract Brown. It was her job, but Camila had other reasons to dislike the girl. She tried to push down the jealousy she always felt around the 6'0", built-like-a-marble-statue woman.

Antonia had never given her a reason to doubt her, but she'd seen the way Giovanna looked at her the few times they'd shared a space. Giovanna had even dared to tell Camila to her face how she didn't understand what Antonia saw in her. It had taken all of her will to not put the stupid goalkeeper in her place. She'd never told Antonia about it. She hadn't wanted to create a conflict between the teammates. But Camila had hated Giovanna ever since, and she couldn't deny it would be so sweet to score a goal against her and celebrate it in her face.

The air caught in her throat when she saw Giovanna lunge in the ball's direction, but Brown had aimed her shot to the corner with enough force the goalkeeper couldn't stop it. It was now 1-0 for the United States in the World Cup Final. That was all they needed. The game had been intense for all 90 minutes, but neither team scored after that.

When the referee blew the whistle marking the end of the game, Camila fell to her knees. She'd done it. They'd done it. Her teammates ran and jumped, screaming with joy all around her, but she couldn't bring herself to join them. She grasped the grass, digging her nails into it until the soil gave in under her fingers. A reminder that indeed, all this was real. She'd dreamed about this moment, but never thought she would actually live it. Hell, weeks before the tournament started, she wasn't even sure they would include her on the team. Over the years, they'd often left her off the USWNT team, no matter how well she was doing at her club. She'd felt bitter about it at first, but she let it go once she realized it had nothing to do with her ability as a player and a lot more to do with politics and maybe even personal grievances by the manager. But she'd been so good this past season they couldn't keep ignoring her, and now...

Now she was a world champion.

She wasn't sure how long she stayed like that. It couldn't have been that long. Someone tumbled into her. Tumbling to the pitch amid a tangle of limbs and laughs, they were soon joined by another teammate, and then another, until they turned into a pile of crying, laughing, hugging women. One by one her teammates got up to continue on their celebratory sprints. Camila lay on the field, a smile on her face staring up at the crystal blue sky.

An extended hand appeared on her line of vision. She craned her neck to confirm what she already knew. Antonia.

The urge to pull Antonia down with her and have her lay beside her was overwhelming, but she stopped it. She took the offered hand and allowed Antonia to help her stand up.

"Hey there, heard you're a world champion now. That's sexy."

Camila chuckled. "I guess I am. Can you believe it?"

"Not really. I can't believe the referee bought that world-class diving you did to get that penalty. I guess that makes you the MVP."

"Shut up," Camila answered, bumping Antonia's shoulder with her own.

She knew Antonia was just trying to rile her up and she couldn't help but laugh. Once upon a time, a comment like that would have brought up all her insecurities and made her explode in anger. Now she could accept the joke.

Camila took off her shirt and stood there in only her sports bra. "Would you swap shirts with me?" she said, offering her jersey to Antonia, who grabbed it without hesitation.

"Of course. You'll have to sign it for me later."

On the surface, exchanging jerseys when they were around each other all the time and planning to share a home soon made little sense. But for Camila, it was the easiest way she had of telling Antonia how much she respected her and how proud she was of the way she'd played all tournament without saying it. It was her way of saying, "I may have won today, but I recognize how good you are." It may also become a good memento of their first World Cup Final. Antonia was right, it didn't matter who won or lost but that they lived the experience together. Having each other's shirts was the perfect way to remember that.

Past midnight Camila heard a knock on the door. She frowned, wondering who would knock that late, but she moved to open the door anyway. Antonia stood outside, dangling a bottle of champagne in front of her face.

"What are you doing here?" Camila asked, a smile taking over her face.

Antonia leaned forward. "I sneaked in," she fake whispered. "Let me in before I get caught," she said.

Antonia stepped inside, her chest pressing against Camila's back when she slid past her. The subtle, innocent touch made Camila close her eyes and take a deep breath that filled her nose with the sweet smell of Antonia. After closing the door, she simply watched Antonia parade around the hotel room without a care in the world. The champagne bottle swung loosely in her hand while she took two glasses from the minibar.

Camila leaned against the door. "What are you doing here?" she asked again, a hint of playfulness in her voice.

"Celebrating, of course."

"Hmmm... is that so?" Camila moved closer to Antonia with measured steps. Her eyes stared right into Antonia's and once she was within reach, Camila wrapped a hand around Antonia's waist and pulled her closer. "It's been too long since the last time I kissed you."

"Then kiss me."

Camila was more than happy to lean down and close the distance between them. The kiss was soft and slow. A simple caress. She wanted Antonia as much as ever. Her core heated with a well-placed touch or a whispered invitation, but she no longer felt the need to take it all at once. The fear had subsided. She was no longer afraid of Antonia leaving or hurting her. She no longer wanted to take everything she could from Antonia at every chance. She was no longer in a rush. Antonia had Camila's heart in her hands, but now Camila trusted her with it.

One kiss turned into two, and then three. It didn't change in intensity. It was a simple coming together of their lips and once they separated, Camila would lean down again for another peck and another.

Antonia hummed and licked her lips. "I guess I'm glad you won. I'd rather kiss you than have you being all grumpy all night."

"I would have been happy for you, if you won." Camila crossed her arms in mock outrage.

Antonia smiled. "Sure, babe."

"OK, I would have been grumpy and in a bad mood for a couple of hours, but then I would have been happy for you," she finally admitted.

Antonia kissed her again. "I know you would have."

"How are you so relaxed? So happy, even though you lost?"

"Way to rub it in."

Camila gave Antonia a pointed look. *Stop the jokes. I want a serious answer.*

"It hurts. I won't say it doesn't. But this is not the end of the road. I have at least a good ten, maybe fifteen more years of professional life. Still plenty of chances to win it." Antonia said. "Not everything has to happen right away."

Camila sighed. "Yeah, sometimes I forget that." She sat on the bed. "I'm sure you'll win the World Cup one day too, and I'm going to be so happy for you."

Antonia sat next to her and grabbed her hand. "I know you will be."

It was scary for Camila to realize she'd never been happier than at that moment. Not because she'd done the thing she'd always wanted to do. Not because she'd won. But because Antonia loved her in a way she'd never felt before. She felt at peace, looking into Antonia's brown eyes, resting in her arms. It had been so hard to accept Antonia's love because even with her parents she'd never known what it was to be loved just for yourself, expecting nothing in return. But now she couldn't imagine being loved any other way.

"Can we cuddle?"

"Of course, champion. Anything you want. Today is your day."

Camila wrapped herself around Antonia's body. She buried her head in her chest and held her tightly. She'd never felt more at peace than in that moment, and she wished she could stay forever in Antonia's arms. Maybe she would.

Receive a free copy of my short story Cartagena Nights as a welcome gift for joining my newsletter at https://johanagavez.com/cartagena

About the Author

Johana is a proud Colombian that loves losing herself in stories and fantasy worlds. She loves watching cooking shows, even though she can barely cook, and spending relaxing afternoons reading in her hammock. At risk of becoming a stereotype, she loves to listen to Shakira, Maluma and J Balvin, but will always choose tea over coffee.

Her writing is centered on Sapphic stories with romance at their core. She loves fluffy novels where love always wins. She reads and would love to write any genre, but romance and mystery hold a special place in her heart.

You can stay in touch with her via e-mail using johana@johanagavez.com or on your favorite social media.

This author is part of iReadIndies, a collective of self-published independent authors of sapphic literature.
Please visit our website at iReadIndies.com for more information and to find links to the books published by our authors.

Lightning Source UK Ltd.
Milton Keynes UK
UKHW012238060223
416577UK00010B/797/J